THE SPECTACULAR LIFE OF
BENITO MARTIN DEL CANTO

by

DAVID TOWNER

ISBN: 979-8-9883530-1-0 (paperback)
ISBN: 979-8-9883530-0-3 (ebook)

Cover Design:

Diego López Mata and Aan Turnip

PROLOGUE

1552

It is a strange, still night, and the rutted road to Seville lies quiet. The land that flanks the trail is patched with yellow grasses that form a plush blanket over the rolling hills.

A lone, predawn traveler is the only exception to the perfect tableau. This boy, only about five years old, walks with a cadence of purpose belonging to a man four times his age.

He stops in his tracks, sensing something ahead. His eyes glide to the left, then the right. His intuition then guides his attention skyward. He is mesmerized.

The sun's appearance in the eastern sky will occur in one hour, eleven minutes, so the darkness of the sky is at its peak. However, the perfect black canvas is disrupted by floating, white specks, slowly descending to earth. As they near, they grow larger and larger. He watches in awe.

Just overhead, he tracks the large white saucers falling to the earth, as peaceful as anything he has ever witnessed. The boy, Benito, fascinated by this magic show, reaches out to catch a snowflake as large as a plate. They seem to absorb all the earth's ambient sound as they blanket the landscape then magically dissolve into the earth.

Benito has never known such silence and tranquility.

Peter is exhausted by the time he arrives at the corner bookshop in Seville. He's never been to this one before, but he's chosen it on recommendation from a business colleague. He knows he looks like a typical American business traveler, and he is ok with that. The suit and rolling suitcase give him away anyway.

Upon entering, his attention is drawn immediately to the vintage books, the well-traveled ones, relegated to the furthest corner of the store as if they are in some sort of literary exile. He maneuvers his suitcase carefully around the pillars of books that rise from the floor. The structural integrity of the stacks is quite marvelous, but he doesn't want to take any unnecessary risks. When he arrives at the desired shelf, he immediately takes note of a particularly weathered book with tons of character.

"That one just gathers dust. You take interest?" Abelardo, the shopkeeper, looks over Peter's shoulder. He's perused the pages many times before, but it's been a while since anyone else has paid any attention to this title.

Peter, suddenly self-conscious, closes the book gently. He stands and reaches to place it back on its dusty shelf. "I'm looking for something for my daughter," he says. "She's twelve and very into authentic Spanish culture."

Abelardo, noticing Peter's fond smile at the mention of his daughter, takes the book from his hand before it can be put back in its place.

"This is as authentic as it gets. Children love it." He looks to the Children's section where a small cluster of youngsters gather around a few picture books. Peter finds his voice to be genuine, not like he's just trying to pawn off an old book.

"Then why is it still on the shelf?" he asks, despite his growing trust in the shopkeeper.

"Perhaps they know they can always find it here," he says with a light shrug. He looks back to the kids, and they look at him this time, giggling briefly before returning to their books. "Plus, they live right upstairs."

Peter nods with a laugh. His grandkids. Of course. "Alright, then." He looks down at his watch. "I'll take it."

Abelardo hands the book back to him with a smile.

Later that afternoon, Peter makes his flight with plenty of time to spare. He always makes sure to get an aisle seat, no matter what it takes. He collapses into his seat and kicks his carry-on bag haphazardly under the seat in front of him. The novel has been slipped into one of the exterior pockets.

Peter falls asleep before the flight even departs. It's been a long week for him. A flight attendant, noticing the bag slipping out into the aisle, nudges the briefcase out of the aisle. When it doesn't budge, she slides it out gently and lifts it into Peter's overhead bin.

The book comes to life.

1547

My name is Benito. Benito Martin del Canto, son of Juan Martin del Canto, and heir to multiple royal lineages. I should preface my story with a humble acknowledgment that many of my tales may seem outrageous, embellished, or fabricated. This is due not to an overactive imagination but a complete lack of skepticism toward the supernatural and an affinity toward adventure and bravery, both of which I inherited from my mother.

My mother was known simply by the name "M," as she was most often in a hurry. It is said that she was always rushing about in an effort to evade bloodhounds, soldiers, and occasionally, beasts of lore, nipping at her heels but never quite catching her. She'd dart across streams and rivers, into large swaths of woods, eventually leaving me behind during one such adventure. It was either me or her own survival. She chose the latter. It was from my mother that I gained my sense of independence, but it was my adoptive family that had the greatest impact on my survival skills.

Though a herd of Iberian mountain goats may not be traditionally regarded of as a suitable family for a human baby, they nurtured me and provided a strong foundation for life. They taught me to stay alert to the presence of predators. They taught me to navigate rocky cliffs in search of food. They taught me to huddle together with others during violent storms.

Life with my adoptive family was neither slow nor fast, exciting nor dull, difficult nor easy. But I was certain that the world had much more to offer me, and I was quite confident that I had much to offer the world. By the age of nine months, seventeen days, I had grown weary of the restrictive, mundane life in the wild and followed my internal compass toward a higher quality life, one filled with substance and excitement.

Peter Michaels arrives home late that night, jetlagged, despite the hours of rest he got on the plane. He enters his humble Boston home weighed down with luggage, drained and still wearing his suit. Yet, he expects his welcoming party will energize him again.

Taryn, the smartest twelve-year-old in the world by her standards and hers alone, drops her current favorite book on Spanish art history and darts downstairs.

"Finally!" She races to him and jumps into his arms. "How was it? Did you see *La Feria de Sevilla*? Did you dance with the local *señoras*?"

Peter smiles as she excitedly twirls and ends in a *flamenco* pose. He laughs a bit, his tiredness showing in his lack of energy, and sets his things down before collapsing on the couch.

"I saw it, but I did not dance," he says, bracing himself for her inevitable frown. "What's been going on with you, kiddo?"

Taryn pouts, her patience wearing thin already. "Nothing interesting. Tell me what YOU did!"

Peter looks at his phone's clock. As much as he loves her, these interrogations when he gets home from his business trips are some of the more difficult moments that come with having a pre-teen daughter. "Taryn," he says slowly. "You have to be up in seven hours for Gloria to take you to school."

Taryn kneels by the couch and folds her arms on his chest. Her lower lip juts out. "Please, please, please?"

Peter looks at her seriously and brushes her hair from her forehead. He can't resist that face. He never could. "Well, I do have something for you."

Taryn's eyes immediately light up. He pulls the book from his briefcase, attempting to conceal it but to no avail.

"Oh, is it a book?!"

His face and body deflate exaggeratedly, feigning sadness that the surprise is ruined, but returns to normal with a smile on his face as he hands Taryn the book. She beams with excitement.

"Where'd you get it? What's it about? Who wrote it?" He smiles down at her, warmed by her joy, but the enthusiasm fills him with weariness after the long day of travel.

"It's just fantasy. Nobody knew who wrote it or seemed to want it. But I guess it plays to a young imagination," he says. He shrugs and ruffles up her hair. She swipes him away, moving her attention to the book in front of her.

"It doesn't really look like a kid's book," she says curiously, toying with the embossed features decorating the spine. She runs her fingers down the exposed pages of the closed tome, quietly daunted by its length, and opens the cover to reveal the handwritten title, alone on its own page: *The Spectacular Life of Benito Martin del Canto.*

She looks up to see Peter staring at his phone. Her stomach pangs lightly, but she still kindles an ember of hope that he will entertain her. She flips to the first page and coughs to get her father's attention before a theatrical reading: "My name is Benito. Benito Martin del Canto–"

Peter gently closes the book. "Time for bed." She dejectedly gets up. His hand tugs at the book, and she lets go. He smiles lightly at her as he finds a place for the book on a nearby shelf. "I know you. You'd be through a hundred pages before breakfast and then asleep in class. We'll talk about school soon, okay? Try to stay on task tomorrow."

Taryn sighs and goes to the stairs, stopping at the top. She looks back, expecting him to follow. Peter looks up from his phone. "Bit more work to do." Taryn shakes her head, blows a kiss, and turns off the light. His phone screen continues to glow.

Gloria pushes the Michaels' front door open with her shoulder, her arms full of their groceries for the week.

"*Hola!*" she screams from the foyer. She looks around upon hearing nothing but silence. Sound always fills the space, even if it's just Peter at the dining room table typing on his laptop. Suspicious, she enters the living room and finds Peter asleep with his phone on his chest. She shakes her head and continues to the kitchen, bringing out eggs, tomatoes, green onions, and flour. She fills a cup with water. After preparing a quick dough and placing it into the oven, she leans down to check on it, smiling happily to herself. She wipes down the counter, flour on her wrinkled finger pads.

Soon, Gloria heads for Taryn's bedroom with a plate in each hand, a freshly sizzled omelet on one and an *ensaimada* on the other. She silently creeps to the bedside, where Taryn snores softly, head turned facing the door. Gloria sneaks the ensaimada beneath Taryn's nose. She awakes groggily, then quickly sits up in bed and reaches for it. Gloria skillfully swings it out of reach before Taryn can snatch it and exits smugly as Taryn quickly runs to her dresser to grab the day's clothes.

Gloria waves the omelet above Peter's face. He doesn't stir, and she considers lightly tapping him on the forehead with the plate. Before she can, his eyes flash open and he jolts up, anxious.

"7:40," says Gloria. "Ten minutes to shower, ten minutes to dress, ten minutes to eat." At that, Peter calms down.

"Thank you, Gloria." She carries the plates to the kitchen and places them on the table, which is already set. She looks back at him.

"No problem, *Señor* Peter."

A dressed-for-the-day Taryn rushes by her dad on the couch, kisses him on the cheek, grabs *Benito* from the shelf, and slides into her chair to eat.

"I guess I'm the only one who needs to get it together," says Peter. Gloria opens the dishwasher.

"Mmmmhm," Gloria responds confidently, a knowing aura always around her. Without looking up from the open book, Taryn nods as well.

1549

In my great expanse of travel, older now, but still just a toddler, I happened upon a monastery. I stopped there, awed by its magnitude and sprawling history, humbled by the knowledge I knew must be held by its dwellers.

I began my formal education as a student in the primary school at the monastery, an institution run by Jesuits. I was the youngest student by many years, a mere toddler surrounded by teenagers. We studied together, and though our teachers were strict, I felt myself thriving in this new type of domestic civilization.

I still recall many of my lessons, especially those in algebra. The Jesuit priests would work at the front of the room, and we'd sit at our desks. Most students would look out the window at the beautiful, distracting countryside or even begin to doze off. But not me. I was always ready for that moment where the teacher would whip around expectantly, waiting for someone to answer the problem he'd drawn out on the board. I knew only blank stares surrounded me, so I'd sigh and raise my hand.

As I rose, the priest would always comment with a smile, "Ah, Benito is brave enough."

But instead of solving the problem at hand, I'd grasp the eraser and clear the middle of the board. I could feel my classmates perk up. Then, I'd jot down a physics equation to explain how one could determine how long until recess based on the angle of the sun visible from the window. The class would be excited, hooting and hollering, but I wouldn't stop there. I'd take it a step further and explain heliocentrism. Before them all, I'd declare that the world would soon accept that planetary orbits must be elliptical.

My presentations would always elicit a standing ovation from all in attendance.

I adjusted quite well to a more domesticated lifestyle, though I found daily existence unrewarding and hardly challenging in any capacity. At the age of two years, seven months, I had absorbed all the knowledge that was available to me in the primary school system. I decided it was time to pursue full-time employment. I had to support myself after all.

At least while I contemplated a greater plan.

I recall standing before the village wall where all available village occupations were listed. I watched the metalsmith hammer away, but the intense heat turned me away quickly. I watched the moneychanger for some time, until I noticed he was adding extra weight to the coin scale to cheat his customers.

Then, one day, a loaf of day-old bread was tossed my way. I caught it. My stomach growled. Salvador Sanchez Du Munon, the baker, smiled at me, bright as day, and returned to his bakery. But when he did, he left the door open for me to follow behind.

Taryn read her book all through the morning, on the way to school and during morning recess. Now, in her classroom, she continues to read. She can't help it.

That is, until a hand slips over her page, and her teacher, Miss Loureiro, takes the book from her. She tries not to draw any attention with her reaction, but the eyes of the class slide towards her. She doesn't like this class anyway.

"I said at the beginning of class that I would take away anything that distracts from the lesson," Miss Loureiro says, a bit apologetically. "Please stop bringing in other things to do during class time."

Taryn looks up at the board. Miss Loureiro had been teaching the names of fruits in Spanish. Boring.

"But it's a Spanish novel," she protests. She should be able to read during class time if she's still learning Spanish.

Miss Loureiro opens it, and Taryn can see that she's clearly a bit intrigued by the antique handwriting on the pages. But as quickly as she does this, the teacher catches herself and closes the book. "You can read this on your own time. It will be on my desk at the end of the day. You can come pick it up then. Now, will you say 'apple' for me?"

"*Manzana*," Caroline says smugly from across the room before Taryn can get a word in. She's always been the teacher's pet. Taryn rolls her eyes as Caroline takes a shiny red apple out of her bookbag and extends it to Miss Loureiro. "For the best teacher ever."

Taryn gags to the freckled kid across the row, who raises his eyebrows in agreement. Caroline flashes a "sweet" smile as Miss Loureiro takes the apple.

"Thank you, Caroline," the teacher says with a smile. "That's really not necessary, but I appreciate the gesture. Please continue with your work. I was asking Taryn."

Taryn grins but then swallows it at Caroline's look of annoyance.

Miss Loureiro turns back to Taryn, but the student responds before she can ask again. "*Las manzanas rojas son el regalo obvio para los maestros, pero sé que prefieres las verdes.*" Red apples are the obvious gift for teachers, but I know you prefer green.

Miss Loureiro cocks an eyebrow in surprise and then bends down close to Taryn. "You can do this. Just a little focus, okay? It's a short class."

With that, she turns back to her desk and places Taryn's book in the drawer. Taryn, bored, begins slowly copying the board.

When the bell rings, the class instantly begins to buzz with happy chatter. The kids drain out for lunch after putting away their school supplies and grabbing their food. After about three minutes of hustle and bustle, Miss Loureiro is left in her quiet classroom, the last student gently closing the door.

She sighs. Another day. They all seem to blend together. She opens a drawer and uncrumples her sack lunch. Not very fancy, but she's never minded that much. She reaches inside and pulls out a Granny Smith apple. She notices, beneath the sack, Taryn's book.

The most interesting thing to come out of today.

She pulls it out and looks over the antique binding in wonder. Where could Taryn have found this? She carefully opens it, her curiosity getting the better of her. She scours the first few pages, looking for some indication of time and place. She finds two tiny initials in the corner of the inside binding: "M.S." For some reason, she feels guilty at having seen it.

Enough of this. She should be working. Her mind races, and then when she sees "1:00" on the clock, it races faster. She puts the book back in the drawer.

She pulls up the internet on her computer, once she revives it, and chews her apple anxiously as she does. She closes her eyes, breathes deep, and then opens her email.

When she opens her eyes, she's met with a rejection letter from the Princeton MA program in Spanish History. Great.

So as not to dwell too much in the dejection, she solemnly closes her email and turns to her students' papers. This is what she's doing now. She should appreciate what her job offers her. She picks up the first paper: Caroline's.

Within seconds, she's furiously marked red pen over countless mistakes. She tries not to channel her frustration at the rejection into her edits, but she can't really help it.

Next is Taryn's. Great. She raises her pen, ready to do damage, but there are no mistakes at all. She sits completely still. Guilt immediately washes over her. She takes a bite out of her apple.

She looks at the apple, a pretty, bright green color, and then back at Taryn's flawless paper.

At the end of the school day, Miss Loureiro resolved that she would try harder to connect with Taryn. Here was a young student, incredibly motivated about the Spanish language, who just didn't enjoy the structure of a formal Spanish class. And that was fine!

When the final bell rings, Miss Loureiro stands at the door, saying goodbye to each student as they leave for the day. Taryn is the last to leave and passes her teacher alone.

"Taryn, wait," Miss Loureiro calls. The student stops. Miss Loureiro jogs a few steps to her and produces the book. "You don't want to forget this."

She smiles earnestly, but Taryn just nods and gives an obviously fake smile. "Thanks."

"I peeped at it a bit. It's really quite fascinating."

Taryn can't figure out what to say, so she just looks at her. Then, she turns and walks away, down the hall and on the way home.

That evening, Peter is still incredibly jetlagged, so they eat a bit earlier than usual. He plans to get to bed as quickly as possible.

At the table, he stuffs a bite of spinach into his mouth. Taryn sneakily texts beneath her plate of spinach and tilapia. Surely, she thinks her father doesn't notice. He does.

"So," he says pointedly. "What happened at school today?"

Taryn doesn't look up. "Nothing interesting."

"Really? Because I heard there was a little drama over the book I gave you."

Taryn looks up now, a bit worried. Had her teacher really told her dad?

Before she can say anything, Gloria walks in and puts a glass of water in front of Taryn. Then, she sets her own plate on the table. She eyes Taryn's untouched food.

"Do you want something else, Taryn?"

Peter motions for Gloria to sit. "No, she will eat this lovely dinner you've prepared, Gloria." He eyes Taryn threateningly, but she's back to texting and doesn't even notice.

"Is there something wrong with it?" Gloria asks Taryn. She's gotten good at ignoring Taryn's father in these situations to really get through to the kid.

"No, Gloria, it's very nice. Thank you." She sighs and looks back at her plate, still not appetized. "Actually, maybe a little salt?"

Peter puts down his fork with a clatter, drawing the gaze of both Gloria and his daughter. "We're getting away from the point. Alice Loureiro told me today that you weren't paying attention to the Spanish lesson yet again. She had to take away 'participation points.'"

"She called you?" Taryn asks, shocked.

"No. We had a scheduled conference this afternoon. She probably wouldn't have said anything if I hadn't noticed your book on her desk."

Taryn shakes her head, looking down to her phone again. "At least she has good taste in literature," she mutters.

"She's a very nice woman," Peter presses. "I don't know why you have to make it so hard for her."

Taryn immediately makes a face. "When did she become the priority?"

Peter takes a deep breath at that and begins to speak very slowly. "You know you are always my priority, but you need to learn that your actions affect other people. Like Gloria, who I'm sure would like to see you eat a little."

Gloria, not focused on the conversation between the two of them at all, continues to eat.

"I'm not going to do everything anyone tells me just because they're older," Taryn says, a slight smile on her face at Gloria's obliviousness. "I'm not a robot. I should be able to call some of my own shots. Why should I listen to Miss Loureiro lecture on something I learned when I was two? I have better things to do with my time."

Peter stifles his frustration. "I–"

"Pass the salt, please."

Peter roughly turns the saltshaker on its side and forcefully rolls it in Taryn's direction. She moves to the side just as it shoots off the table, spilling onto the floor.

This gets Gloria's attention. She stands, but not before Peter does. He jumps up and runs to Taryn, who's a little shaken.

"I'm sorry," he says. They hug each other. "That was way harder than I meant it to be."

Taryn, from over his shoulder, begins to laugh genuinely. Peter starts laughing too. In a moment, the two of them are cackling like banshees.

With a shake of her head, Gloria begins to clean up the broken shaker and salt, laughter still droning in the background.

After dinner has been cleaned, father and daughter decide to work on opposite sides of the couch. Peter has his laptop out, typing away at a memo, and Taryn reviews her homework. They both wear glasses which Gloria finds particularly endearing.

"Alright," Peter says, after finishing a particularly aggressive bout of typing. "Let's hear what this fantastic book is all about."

Taryn looks up, hopeful, and then gleefully pulls out the book and brings it closer to him.

"So far, the main character, Benito, is doing amazing things, even though he's just a baby and a toddler. He already went through school, and he's smarter than his teachers. So now, he's going to town to get a job."

Peter nods at this, not entirely interested, but he tries to remind himself that supporting her enthusiasm is important. She clears her throat. He settles in as she begins to read.

1551

By age four, I had worked my way into a position of great responsibility at the bakery owned by Salvador Sanchez Du Munon, who, for reasons still unknown to me, preferred to be called Santiago. He was a well-known and respected man throughout the village of Seville, not just for his superior pastries but for his kindness and generosity. Visiting Spanish noblemen often came, dressed richly with their haughty smiles and curling black mustaches, and each time, he offered them fardelejos. The noblemen would easily accept this gift. Poor children, too, grew to love Santiago and the basketfuls of bread he would offer them.

But Santiago was still a man, and he was restricted by that very humble nature that made him an icon of his community. When Turkish coffee beans came to our land, he refused them, confused by what these new salesmen were selling. He also had the misfortune of never traveling beyond the confines of Seville. We watched men leave for the "New World" from the comfort of our doorway. We offered them bread but never traveled alongside their dreams.

I began painting to visualize the memories of my life. I told Santiago the story of my birth through these paintings, my childhood in the mountains with my adoptive family, hunting wild game in Africa, and my stint as a goat herder in Tibet just before joining him at the bakery. I painted the ocean and coiled seashells. Once I told him of the ocean, he wanted it described to him over and over. He taught me to make ensaimadas which looked just like the seashells in my paintings.

Still, no matter how much I tried to tell him of the world that lived outside the bakery walls, he seemed content to live a life of adventure vicariously through my experiences.

At times, Santiago did seem skeptical of my history and motives. Yet he was always willing to accommodate my unusual requests because I was such a dedicated and hard worker. In one such example, he allowed me 12 baguettes per day to feed to the fire-breathing dragons that lived just beyond the village.

I climbed a steep cliff to get to them, following a path I knew well. I continued until I reached the opening of a cave. When I made it there, I tossed the baguettes Santiago had given me into its depths. Then, I turned on my heel and walked away as quickly as I could, the sound of ravenous beasts fighting over the bread becoming louder and louder behind me.

It's quite fortunate Santiago allowed me to complete this quest, as these daily baguettes were the only staple keeping these terrible *beasts from entering the village and consuming the good, hard-working people of Seville. In my old age, I have yet to understand people like Santiago who dispute claims of facts that are easily proven. I invited him to feed the dragons with me many times, but each time, he declined. I can only deduct that skeptics are just happy being skeptics. It's fortunate that there are people like me in the world, those willing to dedicate their lives to keeping societies safe from unseen dangers, famine, disease, marauders, malevolent creatures, various hardships, and other misfortunes, even if it's an uncelebrated and unrewarded existence.*

The only reward I knew during that time was that of climbing the cliffs, finding new viewpoints from which to overlook beautiful Seville.

"Fire-breathing dragons?" Peter asks, incredulous.

Taryn shushes him. "It's interesting."

"I'm glad you like it, but it's just fantasy, you know. When I finally take you to Spain, I don't want you to be disappointed because you romanticized it."

"When?!" Taryn's eyes immediately light up at the thought.

"I'm not sure yet–"

"Well, I–"

Peter didn't want Taryn to get her hopes for Spain too high. He didn't have anything on the books yet, and his calendar was pretty packed for the foreseeable future. He didn't need her pestering him about it right now. So, he decides to change the subject back to the actual book.

"This fellow certainly thinks highly of himself."

"Well," Taryn says, leaning back against the couch. "He saved the village from dragons. At five years old."

"Oh yes, of course. My apologies. Please continue." Taryn can't tell if he's teasing her or not.

"'Just happy being a skeptic,'" she breathes.

Peter hears and playfully ruffles her hair. She smiles at this but then pushes him away before composing herself. She looks at him incredulously above her glasses, then pushes them farther up her nose.

"Continue," he says, gentler this time. "Seriously."

Taryn's smile softens, and she settles back into her place on the page. Before she even begins to read, she can feel her father dozing off next to her. She kisses him lightly on the head and continues to read.

1552

Of all the experiences of my life, none were met with more skepticism than the one that occurred on the very day I turned five years of age. I was walking to Seville to open the bakery and prepare the dough as I always did. Exactly one hour, eleven minutes prior to the sun's appearance in the eastern sky, my senses drew my attention to the heavens. Out of the clear sky, large white saucers began to descend to the earth, as peaceful as anything I had ever witnessed. I reached out to catch one as large as a plate, but it turned to water before my very eyes. They fell all around me, blanketing the empty countryside.

They seemed to absorb all the earth's ambient sound. I had never known such silence and tranquility. As clear as my words appear before you here, those saucers, larger than a grown man's fist, fell upon the soil and descended into the earth.

"Hello, children!" Principal Kelly enters the classroom and parades through the aisles. Taryn has never cared much for him.

He looks harmless enough, a slightly chubby man in a cheap suit, but she still finds him a bit creepy. When he enters, Taryn hides her book beneath her desk just in time.

"What a beautiful day!" Principal Kelly proclaims, arms spread wide. "Are you all studying your little hearts out?"

He smiles, but the students in the cluster of desks around him all move away slightly. All except for Caroline.

"Why, yes, Principal Kelly!" Caroline beams, and Principal Kelly pats her on the head.

"What a good girl, Caroline." He seems as though he's about to continue until he notices Taryn in the front corner. "Taryn, I have heard so much about you and your voracious reading lately."

He goes to ruffle her hair, and she winces at the contact. Miss Loureiro notices and comes over as quickly as possible.

"What can I help you with, Principal?" Her voice is stern which draws an incredulous look from the principal. He lifts his hand from Taryn's head innocently.

"Oh, Alice. I know Taryn well enough to know she wouldn't be offended by a little pat on the head." He kneels down and puts his and Taryn's heads together with a light push. Miss Loureiro watches him make a puppy dog face and shakes her head. "Are you completely against any physical contact with these children who may be starved of it at home?"

At this, Taryn is finally fed up. She gives a visible scowl and pulls her head from the principal's. "I am–"

But she's met with a warning look from Alice that stops her from saying any more. As if on cue, Miss Scarry peeks her head in the door.

"Principal Kelly!" Miss Scarry wails. The squeaky, slim, and frantic secretary is just about everyone's least favorite person on campus. The entire class turns toward her voice, and Miss Loureiro rolls her eyes so only Taryn can see. When Principal Kelly doesn't budge, she squeaks again, louder this time. "It's serious!"

He makes an exaggerated sigh, disappointed that his little drama has been interrupted. "Miss Loureiro, would you join me outside?"

With an apologetic look toward Taryn, she gives a nod of agreement. "Okay." Together, all of them walk out into the hallway, leaving the class of children to eavesdrop.

"What?" Principal Kelly says once the door closes behind him. "This'd better be good."

Miss Scarry looks even more afraid, if that was even possible. "Taryn…Taryn Michaels? Her father got in a car accident this morning. He's unconscious."

Alice Loureiro gasps. She can't help herself. "Is he going to be ok?" She feels like she's seeing stars.

In lieu of response, Miss Scarry just nods and takes down everything that's been said so far, including Miss Loreiro's gasp. Alice feels frustration boiling up.

Before she can say anything, Miss Scarry continues, looking this time at Principal Kelly. "So, the girl has to be told…"

The principal puts a hand up to stop her. "I hardly know the girl. What was her name again?"

"Taryn," Miss Loureiro fills in, her eyes squeezed shut.

"Yes, Taryn," Principal Kelly says, entirely butchering the pronunciation of the name. "Your student, if I'm correct, Miss Loureiro? I think this is the perfect opportunity for you to shine as more than a teacher – a personal mentor, even. And ASAP."

Miss Loureiro's jaw nearly drops as she looks at him in disbelief. This is the task of a school therapist, not of an instructor of Spanish language. When Miss Scarry finishes scribbling, the two administrators look at Alice expectantly.

How ridiculous. Without another word, Miss Loureiro takes a step back into the classroom and shuts the door.

When Taryn reaches the hospital room, Gloria is there waiting for her, juice bottle in hand. This doesn't stop Taryn from crying – she's been unable to stop the tears since Miss Loureiro told her – but it does make her feel a little less alone. Alice, actually. Miss Loureiro had asked to be called Alice now.

Taryn sits in the chair by Peter's bedside and immediately puts her hands over her face. Gloria rubs her back for a moment. Then, deciding that the girl would probably like some alone time with her father to process, she exits. Taryn sighs deeply then and uncovers her tear-stained face.

Looking at her father, his eyes closed, is painful. She can't do it.

"Let's keep going in our book, okay?" she says with a shaky voice.

She pulls the Spanish novel out of her backpack. When she opens it, a tear falls on the page. She reaches for a tissue and uses it to dab at her eyes. Then, she begins to read once more, transporting the two of them somewhere that isn't this horrible Boston hospital. No matter the drama in the pages, Peter remains still and silent before her. She puts one hand over his and reads anyway.

1555

By the time I had reached the age of eight years, four months, my great country was advancing toward a golden age of literary and artistic wonderment, global exploration, financial prosperity, and social and intellectual enlightenment.

Naturally, the human instinct leans toward jealousy and there were many other empires that sought to cease our progress and take that which we had rightfully earned. To defend Spain against marauders, tyrants, pilferers, dark forces, and generally undesirable sorts, a call went out to able-bodied men who desired to preserve our motherland and earn a few silver pieces in the meantime.

I bid farewell to Santiago, promising to return one day with more stories of my new adventures. During my journey, I happened upon a pier, a great ocean, ships and sailors, and materials heading to and fro. I've always felt an affinity for the sea, and so I decided to enlist in the naval services.

I stood in line at age eight with all those adult men, proud and patient, and answered questions before the lone man behind the desk.

Yet, when I was sent to the naval enlistment clerk, he eyed me with intensity. He crouched over my documents for a moment and then looked again up at me. Then, with a flourish, he proclaimed, "Unfit for sea duty! Next."

I was shuffled away. Yet, instead of feeling disappointed, I had a smile on my face, even as I was being roughly escorted away from the clerk's desk.

"What an unfortunate decision for you, sir," I said, my voice even and leveled. "And for all of you! I am the best sailor candidate available for active service. I shall see you again but under less cordial circumstances."

The other candidates, amused, began to clap and cheer for me.

Peter's hand makes a tiny movement beneath Taryn's. She stops reading suddenly, shocked at this. She rubs his hand gently, hoping.

Nothing more happens. Gloria enters the room and looks at Taryn expectantly. It's time to go. Taryn thinks for a moment that she should tell Gloria what she felt, but she immediately thinks better of it. She doesn't want to give Gloria any kind of false hope. Taryn knows what she saw. She'd tell a professional.

She stands to leave. Before she does, she turns back just for a moment to see her dad, still peaceful and still on the hospital bed.

The next day, they return to sit at Peter's bedside again. Taryn enters and takes the bedside chair. She excitedly looks up at Peter as soon as she sits down, half-expecting some kind of movement at her arrival. She doesn't want to miss anything.

"I told the doctor about how you moved your hand yesterday," she says gently. "He said it would be 'amazing' if you woke up. I think it'll happen. I have faith in you."

She pulls the book out of her bag and begins to tear up just looking at the cover. She tries not to get too choked up and looks back up at her dad, pressing her hands against the book. She then reaches for his hands and does the same to them, laying them lightly against the cover.

"I believe this book. Amazing things do happen. You'll see," she says in a low whisper.

Then, she opens the book and, once more, begins to read.

1555

Rejection has always been my greatest inspiration. I was not deterred by what had happened, not at any length. I walked along the pier, my sack full of supplies with me, until I found my way.

I spent the next few weeks working at the shipyard in exchange for some supplies and a boat. All the boys of the shipyard became brothers, so in-sync in body and mind. We hammered spokes into huge planks of wood, building ships together, hammering in rhythmic unison. Whenever the overseer called for a break, we would set aside our mallets, wipe our brows, take swigs of water, and begin to chat.

I often remember speaking to a workman on one such break, named Luis.

"So, 'Benito,' is it?" Luis asked me.

"Benito Martin del Canto, son of Juan Martín del Canto." I always said my name with this kind of pride.

"Charming," he nodded, his thoughtfulness clear on his stony face. "Why would a seemingly titled lad such as yourself be swinging this job?"

"I'm forming my own Spanish naval fleet," I said matter-of-factly.

Luis laughed obnoxiously, leading the other workmen around us to start listening.

"You can't just do that!" Luis said.

"And why not?"

"Gold. This wood…" He wrapped his knuckles around the plank we'd been working on. "Do you know how many reales this costs alone? And how much of this you would need for just one ship? You might have some blue blood, but you sure don't look like you bleed gold."

I found myself unfazed by his declarations, though they seemed to persuade his friends. "It's not about a show of wealth," I said. "I aim to protect Spain's interests abroad."

"Abroad?" Luis said, his voice curious now.

"The New World," I confirmed. "I'm tracing the steps of Magellan, leaving from this here Port of Seville, just as he did. But I intend to further explore the vast possibilities of our globe, in the name of Spain."

Everyone around us hushed at this. My new friend, Luis, narrowed his eyes.

"Would any of you brave gentlemen like to join my fleet?" I said, my confidence growing with the lack of pushback from the men.

An old spindly fellow raised his fist. "Better than this job!"

I grinned a bit. A couple more excited affirmations were delivered from the men.

Before I could continue, the overseer's voice rang out over the crowd. "All right then! Let's lay out the next row."

The excitement I had been building tapered off, and the workmen returned to laying out planks of wood to be hammered together. The chatter stopped for the most part, all except for the talk between Luis and another man.

"And what about you, Roderigo?" Luis said. "Where are you from?"

"I'm from here," Roderigo said with a sharpness.

Luis nodded and joined the others in quietly straightening the rows of wood. "Gotta ask now with this Peace of Augsburg business," he muttered under his breath. "Any state in the Holy Roman Empire could be Lutheran if the Prince so chooses!"

"By the Emperor's decree," I said, and a couple of other men jeered and muttered angrily.

"Sometimes, I wonder if he loves peace more than Spain," Luis said with a shake of his head.

A couple of men gasped at that.

"As long as he is our ruler, we will honor his law," the elderly man responded.

A younger workman from down the line chimed in also. "It may not be long. If Phillip II leads us, Spain will remain strong. Strength is in the Catholic faith, not tolerance of heresy."

The overseer, oblivious to the conversation at hand, drew near once again. "Alright," he said. "Let's be done for the day. Blessings on All Saint's Day tomorrow."

This was met with cheers from all the workmen.

"Everyone head to Triana," Luis responded. "I know some great flamenco girls. Tonight still belongs to the living!"

After everyone had gathered their things and prepared to depart, we met outside the entrance to the shipyard. All the workmen happily gathered around Luis, ready to go, except for myself and Roderigo. We prepared to leave in the other direction.

"Aren't you gathering with your families?" Luis asked the two of us.

"I can't very well make it to the Vatican by Vespers tomorrow."

Luis smiled, impressed and a bit amused. "Alright. Roderigo?"

Roderigo looked up with his usual blank expression. "My family has recently gone to the desert lands. Only I remain in Seville."

"Lutherans," another workman muttered.

The elderly man shut him up with an elbow to the ribs. "Cuius regio, eius religio. In the Prince's land, the Prince's religion. Roderigo stayed in a Catholic state; therefore he must be a faithful Catholic."

Luis folded his arms together and leaned back slightly. "Well, I've certainly never seen him with a rosary, that's for sure."

The air grew tense, so tense men could hardly move at all. Luis fingered his work mallet.

Then, I spoke up. "Article 24 of The Peace of Augsburg states, 'In case our subjects, whether belonging to the old religion or the Augsburg Confession, should intend leaving their homes in order to settle in another, they shall not be injured in their honor.' Let us not waste time. Come now, who will meet me in two days' time to set sail for the New World?"

Luis' eyes all of a sudden became less friendly and more filled with contempt. He turned to exit the shipyard, the crowd following.

Rejection has, however, always been my greatest inspiration. I was not deterred, not at any length.

Roderigo and I stood awkwardly then, the two of us alone in the shipyard that was now growing very dark, our packs slung over our shoulders.

"There goes my crew of adventurers," I mused, loud enough for Roderigo to hear. "Well, I am as well-off on my own."

"Benito," Roderigo turned towards me then, his eyes suddenly animated. "You are a brave lad. With no gold and no crew, you are prepared to sail for the New World. However, that burly fellow was wrong. Your problem is not your lack of funds. A civilian cannot sail under the flag of Spain without royal approval. When you set sail, you can hoist nothing but your undergarments without being arrested by the Royal Navy."

I chuckled at that, finding it quite funny. I thought to perhaps tell him of all that I'd tried in regard to the Royal Navy, but I thought better of it. I sighed.

"Come with me," Roderigo said, with a grin.

When we arrived at Roderigo's townhouse, I was quite stunned. It was a beautiful place, well-appointed and colored by expensive decor. I hadn't seen anything like it firsthand. I had to hold back many questions.

"How gracious, Roderigo," I said instead. I looked to the desk to my left and ran a hand lightly over its surface. "Quite tasteful, I must say. French beech?"

Roderigo nodded with a smile. He waved me over to a large plinth chest with beautiful, intricate carvings along its lid. I could've spent a full week examining those carvings, all masterful and detailed. He opened the chest then and sifted through various documents and treasures. Finally, after a couple minutes, he produced a shield with a Spanish knight's crest.

"You may use my crest to sail as a Spanish fleet of Royal order," he proclaimed.

I was stunned, nearly into silence. Once I found my voice again, I didn't have any idea where to start. "You are a knight."

"Not in any sense of importance," he said, his modesty clear in his stance now.

"What! Have you no desire for the greatness you are destined for?" I think of all that I would do if I were a knight, given such an honor by a Royal.

"Many a fool was made of knights. Compelled by whimsies, they imagined chivalry. The shipyard saves me from such frivolities. I like to make something useful for the Crown with my hands." He spoke quietly and calmly, in such a way that one could not even imagine arguing with him.

"'Tis noble in its own way, Roderigo."

Roderigo nodded at this and then offered the shield to me.

"The knightly orders of Spain are dying," he said solemnly. "And I don't think it a bad thing at all. For what it's still worth, you may have it."

"But it's your blood," I said, by way of final protest.

"Do you have room in your fleet?" he asked with the full earnestness of his nature. "I shall be your humble squire of the sea."

I smiled. "You shall be my right-hand man."

We began immediately, Roderigo and I. We packed our bags full of supplies and prepared ourselves for adventure. Our boat was rickety and wooden, no more than 20 feet in length. Still, even alongside a Navy ship, it was most suited for our tasks. The Navy's preparations looked amateur next to ours.

It was quite fortuitous that the naval service turned a blind eye to my talents, I began to realize. I was not the sort to spend months cleaning, preparing, and testing. There was a job to be done, *our exploration, and there was no time to waste. Roderigo provided the flag, emblazoned with a Royal crest, and I hoisted it high. Then, we set sail.*

In 1560, we fought pirates together in the Caribbean, back-to-back, covering each other from all danger. There was always a need for protection of Spain's assets. But what was good for Spain and what was greed? These lines blurred far from the Crown in the wild New World.

As we approached the coastline, all these questions approached us also. Roderigo and I took our "Naval fleet" to see what treasures could be uncovered and what friends could be made in Ponce de Leon's slice of paradise, La Florida. But we led those with less than friendly intentions there unknowingly. The Spanish Naval Fleet had followed us all the way from Spain. They were led by Pedro Menéndez de Avilés. He was courageous. I'll give him that.

Roderigo and I became good friends with the Admiral's son, who accompanied the expedition. We laughed around the bonfire together, sharing stories of our travels. But Diego began a serious flirtation with one of the young French ladies of nearby Fort Caroline. Both Roderigo and I knew to be worried at his pursuit of this girl.

When de Avilés returned to King Phillip II's court, he lied and claimed that his son had been shipwrecked. He kissed the King's hand and relayed this news with a sad expression on his face. He used the King's pity to provide him with all the ships and gold he needed, not to search for his son, but to fulfill much bigger, bloodier plans.

One night in 1565, the Admiral's ships fired cannons at the French Fort Caroline. Explosion after explosion rang throughout the night. The eventual crackle of fires signaled a sure collapse of the fort. I was not concerned with the fort, however. I was thinking only of Diego as Roderigo and I watched from a nearby hilltop where we had made camp. Neither of us were able to watch and brought our attention back to the map we were drawing of the geography between Florida and Spain. As we worked, I cried for my friend, who was sure to burn in his lover's arms by his own father's hand. I cried because I had led them all to this enchanted peninsula with my superior navigation skills, never dreaming of the consequences.

The next day at school, Taryn begins her day by copying Benito's words neatly onto a little pink sheet of paper: *Rejection has always been my greatest inspiration.*

As if on cue, Principal Kelly decides to enter the room.

"Hello, kiddies!" he declares, arms open wide.

"Hello, Principal!" Caroline shoots up out of her chair and waves.

"Caroline," Kelly gestures to her and walks closer. "How is your parents' benefit coming together?"

"Splendidly, thank you," she says, her voice shrill and proud.

Taryn closes her book, hearing the Principal drawing closer to her, and is about to hide it under her desk when he spots her.

"Taryn." He jaunts over to her, already scolding her. "What's on the menu for our hearty reader, hm?"

He snatches up the book with one swift motion. The pink paper with the quote written on it flutters to the floor a few feet away. He begins to stroke the book gently with his hand. "Ooh, soft–"

Alice puts out her left hand instinctively to stop him from touching the book. One must be careful with old books like that. Yet, as she does, Kelly gently takes hold of her hand and lowers it.

Alice is furious. Principal Kelly holds onto her hand until she pulls it away.

"Carry on, lovelies," he says before turning to leave, taking the book away with him.

The moment he's gone, Alice turns to her student. "Taryn–"

Taryn wipes away an angry tear. At that exact moment, the school bell rings. Before Alice can apologize or say anything more, Taryn leaves. When she's gone, Alice notices the pink piece of paper and picks it up off the floor.

She brings it over to her desk which, not surprisingly, has her rejection letter pulled up on the screen of her computer. Just below the rejection is one glowing word that stands out to her: "waitlist." She smooths her thumb over the pink paper.

Rejection has always been my greatest inspiration.

The hospital room seems much drearier to Taryn now that she doesn't have the book to accompany her. She sits in her usual chair, but she has nothing to do now, beyond listening to the beeps of the machines. She stands after a few minutes, frustrated.

"This place is horribly boring," she says, her frustration evident in the hard edge of her tone. "Are you so bored in here? They say you'll be here for who knows how long."

Her father doesn't answer. She's met with only beeps. She wipes away a tear she hadn't even noticed falling.

"Or is your imagination just going crazy? Maybe it's way better here than it is out there."

Again, no answer. She strokes his hand gently and then goes to unzip her backpack. Her talking is the only thing keeping the space from feeling empty, so she continues.

"I thought I'd read to you. I think you liked the Spanish novel, but that awful Principal Kelly took it away today." She pauses for just a moment and then goes on. "I know, I shouldn't have been reading in class. Predictable me. Predictable principal. Predictable lecture from you. You needn't even be conscious for me to hear it in my ears."

She pulls out a stack of library books and spreads them on the edge of the bed. She stands back for a moment, scanning through her options with her eyes.

"I brought all kinds of stuff. There must be something else you want to hear." She picks one up. "What about this – it's a Kennedy biopic. Your favorite. 'Not just a man, not just a leader. The face of America the whole world watched, and the face a wife and four children knew by heart, hardly better than a nation.'"

She thumbs her way over hundreds of pages until the back cover of the tome closes again. It seems interesting enough, but she can't bring herself to start reading. She doesn't feel that same excitement.

"I guess we already know the ending for Kennedy," she says with a sigh. "That's what keeps me going, the thrill of finding out what happens next. These all seem too real…I don't know. Whatever that means."

Renewed in her frustration, she puts the books all back in her bag, zips up the backpack, and heads out the door, letting it slam loudly behind her.

The following day, Taryn returns. When she enters the room once more, a young nurse is finishing tucking in new sheets over Peter's motionless body. The nurse clearly takes a moment to admire Peter's handsome face, and Taryn stares silently as she does this. After a moment, the nurse notices the child's presence and smiles with a mixture of embarrassment and pity. Then, she turns to leave.

Taryn closes the door and plops down into the chair beside the bed, slumping her backpack onto the floor.

"I decided I should take advantage of the situation," she says, speaking quickly, one thought after the next. "You never have much time to listen to me, so I have some notes about what I want to tell you, now that you're ready to listen."

She puts on her glasses and takes out her notepad where she's jotted down sentences in messy cursive.

"Since you always ask, here's the story of my day. But not the boring one." She takes a deep breath and nods before she begins. "The day started with excruciating pain in my stomach because I was starving. Literally. Gloria has not fed me since you've been in here. Now, this is especially dangerous because I'm a growing girl. My growing pains have been getting worse and worse. It's possible that my bones will just shoot through the skin and people will run from me in fear for the rest of my life."

She flips the page of the notepad and continues, growing in confidence and lessening in speed.

Alice sits at her desk during lunch break. She'd been increasingly less motivated to work during her lunch break following the events concerning Taryn. That poor kid. Today, she scrolls through her most recent research interest: methods of dating printing books from the 1500-1700 era.

She clicks a link about the evolution of the novel that looks particularly interesting. It mentions that the first modern novel is widely considered to be *Don Quixote*, by M.C.S: Miguel de Cervantes Saavedra.

She's intrigued. Her intrigue is interrupted, however, by a phone call from the office. Principal Kelly is paging her.

She enters his office slowly, wishing that she could come up with some excuse to avoid this meeting altogether. Kelly, feet on his desk, tosses aside whatever magazine he's been reading. Probably something inappropriate. Alice wouldn't be surprised.

"There we are," he declares in his usual fashion as she enters.

She tries not to show her annoyance in her tone. "You wanted to see me?"

"Yes." He gestures to the bean bag chair across from him. "Have a seat, my dear Alice."

She squeaks into the chair. It's degradingly low to the ground. This just gets worse by the minute. "What's this about?"

He strokes his chin, a mockery of someone in deep thought. "I've been thinking about the trouble you've been having keeping your students' attention."

Alice gulps. The idea of being fired immediately floats through her mind. She squashes it.

"I thought, this is really the parents' fault," he continues, causing her to relax and become confused. "Parenting is the parents' job. And isn't parenting making children follow rules of social decency? Like looking your authority figure in the eyes when they impart invaluable knowledge?"

He does a two-finger "look me in the eye" gesture and then goes to brush his comb-over down. Alice watches him. He notices.

"But unfortunately, some of our most troublesome students, like…" He seems to forget who he's referring to for a moment and then remembers. "Like Taryn Michaels. I've been calling her father, to see if he can shape her up, but these parents…so unresponsive."

"Peter Michaels is in a coma," Alice says, her disgust showing in her tone. She's completely floored.

Kelly waves this off as if it's nothing. "I guess that's as good an excuse as any. Oh, but that Caroline Sweeney? What a delight. She gave me this apple. And a seat at her parents' benefit."

He obnoxiously takes a bite out of the shiny red apple, squirting juice all over. He winks then and sets the half-eaten apple on top of Taryn's book on his desk. Alice eyes it.

"That book…"

"Yes," Alice says, her eyes narrowing. "Taryn Michaels' book."

He picks it up, letting the apple roll off onto the floor. Miss Scarry leans as far as possible through the window into his office, picks up the apple, and then retreats. "You have interest in this book?"

Alice adjusts in her bean bag chair. She attempts to smooth her skirt with dignity, but it's near impossible. "And you have interest in a date for the Sweeney benefit."

Kelly's eyes widen in surprise, and then he recovers his cool moments later. "You're free, then?"

"I can be," Alice says through gritted teeth.

"Saves me a few bucks." He grins.

When Alice exits the room, she has the book triumphantly under her arm.

1567

After everything that happened in La Florida, I decided to work inside the system to see what good I could do. Roderigo took a naval clerk position on land, and I took the lowest position on the finest ship of the Spanish Armada. I was twenty years old, and I mopped the deck as we patrolled the western coast of Africa.

One day, somewhere in the middle of our journey, we heard the bell and a cry from the crow's nest.

"It's not one of Henry Caravel's ships, but I can't decipher her title!" the sailor proclaimed.

The entire crew began to ready the ship for battle. I, on the other hand, was not so quick to fight. I simply stared intently at the strange ship in the distance. Right beside where I had been mopping was the Captain's quarters, and at the sound of the bell, the Captain swung open his door.

"What's all this, boy?" he asked me.

"A strange ship on the horizon," I said, pointing. The man took to his spyglass and peered at the ship. "But I'm not convinced she means to fight. She doesn't even have any petereros."

The Captain nodded curtly to me. "Halt!" he bellowed. All the men on the ship immediately stopped their movement. "Stand down, gentlemen. Return to your ease. It's just the Madre de Deus. Hawkins is sailing her under the flag of Britain. She is of no interest to us."

The preparations for fighting immediately were retracted, and the crew returned to routine maintenance with sighs abound. The Captain stopped me from returning to my mopping. He held out his spyglass for me to look through.

"What is her interest in?" I asked, noting the unique features of the ship.

The Captain took back his spyglass and looked down. "Human cargo," he said before he exited towards his quarters.

"Human cargo," I said, bewildered, as I continued to stare at the foreboding ship. I'd never seen one like it before.

An old Second Mate with one eye and a gold tooth was scrubbing a barrel nearby. He'd been listening in. "You know, the dark skins from the interior."

At that moment, I was made privy to the inner workings of the most evil institution in the history of mankind. I watched the slave ship pass and begin to sail away. With a sudden burst of determination, I climbed onto the ship rail heroically and dived into the waves. The old Second Mate, who had much wanted to *continue the conversation, was surely quite confused that I was gone.*

I gracefully propelled myself through the peaceful, empty ocean. I smiled often, seeing the fish swimming by me on all sides. Eventually, I saw the rudder of the ship and raged toward it with renewed energy, the fish all following. Then, they vanished. I turned around then to see a huge shape approaching me.

A huge shark.

It opened its jaws, a gaping cavern of teeth coming right toward me. I gulped and raced the remainder of the way toward the ship. Then, I leapt toward the hull, jumping off the rudder out of the water and dive-rolling into a low, open porthole.

I set a world record, holding my breath. But when I dove into that porthole, I dove into an atrocity against nature.

The ship lurched violently, hit by the shark's nose. The crowd, made up of dozens of African people, was frightened. When I regained my balance, I noticed the long chain connecting all of them, chaining them to the walls of the hull.

"Prepare to free yourselves, friends," I said. "Carry it up together. I'll provide distraction."

I could hear the ire of the Slave Captain above. He began to descend the stairs.

One woman replied to me in broken Spanish, "We will still be chained if we are above!"

The Slave Captain entered then, and I hid behind a basket of cloth below the porthole.

"What's happening?" he asked the woman. "Is this some kind of black magic?"

Wind blew through the porthole, making a whistling sound. An idea came to me. I seized the top white cloth from the basket and let it blow in the wind as I made eerie ghost noises. The woman looked at me like I was crazy, but I watched the Slave Captain's attention get drawn by the sheet. He walked over to me slowly, clearly a bit nervous. When he got close enough, he snatched it and, pulling on it, pulled me to my feet.

"A navy swab!" He groaned as he dragged me by my collar, up the stairs and onto the deck. He didn't catch me giving a signal to the bewildered people below.

Above, I was thrown into the middle of a ring of scary sailors.

"Now," the Slave Captain said, his eyes fiery with rage. "What to do with you…I suppose you are only a lad. We needn't make this painful. You can swab our deck until we port."

"I'm here because the people below should be free." I've never been one to hide my true intentions.

"Have it your way, insolent traitor," he grumbled. His eyes scanned the crowd, searching for ideas, until he heard a loud splash by the side of the ship. The First Mate looked over the rail.

"Captain…" he said, his voice frightened. The Slave Captain dragged me over until he and I could see what the First Mate was looking at. A huge fin was weaving about below. The Slave Captain smiled maliciously.

"String him up!"

Before I could think of much else, I was bound and dangling from a rope tied to a fishing apparatus and swung out over the water. The Captain and crew seemed to have very much fun watching gleefully over the side of the deck. A huge shark fin was only a dozen yards away, moving ever closer to me.

I looked to the hatch door, the one that led to the galley. No sign of people. The fin came slowly closer. I began, for the first time in my life, to feel a bit nervous.

Then, the hatch door opened. One of the men who I recognized peered out, seeing the crew lined up against the rail with their backs turned. I gave them a nod of encouragement. The man led all the people, carrying their long chain, out onto the deck.

Then, the shark jumped out of the water. The Slave Captain turned and noticed the chained crowd behind him with a yell. And I, well, I was swallowed whole by the leaping shark.

I could hear the screams of everyone onboard from within the shark's belly. When I saw them again, the shark had made another leap, its mouth wide open, showing its rows of shiny white teeth. I could count them. 300. I stood on its tongue, triumphant, as though riding from the inside.

"Hold up your chains!" I yelled. The crowd listened and followed quickly, just in time. The shark leapt one final time, over the ship entirely. As it did, I tumbled onto the deck. The shark crushed its jaws around the chains, breaking all the people free.

The crew ran all directions in fear as the newly freed crowd cheered victoriously. The shark flopped around the deck, chasing and chomping at whatever members of the crew it could find. Before it could get its jaws around any of them though, I put a stop to everything, the violence, and the rejoicing.

"Wait! We need them!" I hollered to the shark. It immediately stopped and leapt off the edge of the boat, into the sea. I watched as it swished off into the sunset with its huge fin zigzagging around. The freed crowd and I waved farewell.

The tides turned after that. I oversaw the crew as they took care of operations on the ship. The Slave Captain was put in charge of swabbing the deck. He did a great job. The newly freed woman took charge of the wheel, bringing the ship all the way around in the direction of their home. I was grateful for the moment of peace, sailing with my face to the wind.

My joy at freedom for my new friends was sublime, but short-lived. As soon as I had traveled to the next port to meet up with my naval crew, I could not help but think of all the people in slavery yet. They haunted my dreams. Now that I had personally experienced a taste of injustice, I was familiar with the pain of physical restraint, but most tortuous, the restraint of the mind. As I saw the horror of slavery grow, my mind raced to the point of lunacy.

I was done with the sea.

In my past, I had been a man of spontaneous action, but in later years, I was making a conscious effort toward rational behavior in order to be free from foolishness and to be taken more seriously by those who influenced my freedom, among other things. In 1570, I found myself thinking of this among the city dwellers of Madrid. I imagined the New World, the horror of the slaves who harvested cotton in vast fields. My vivid imagination has often been my greatest foe, and this scenario was no exception. That night, in 1570, I stood before the Palacio Real de Madrid. *As I visualized the taking of a man from his home, his wife, his children, and his bed, my inclination toward reasonable decisions had met a most formidable enemy: my vivid imagination and its commitment to justice.*

I expertly scaled the wall toward a little window and hopped inside the palace. It was surprisingly easy to enter the King's quarters. Once inside, I looked to the King's grand bed in the lavish room. Oddly, his covers were undone and empty.

Suddenly, a sword swung through the air, slicing at my belly. I deftly grabbed a silver tray from underneath a nearby tea set to defend myself against the strike, leaving all the ceramic elements of the tea set perfectly in their place behind me. The bearer of the sword was King Phillip II, in his nightshirt and stocking cap. He breathed heavily with the sword in his hand, one that he had very clearly pulled off the wall.

"Benito?" He recognized me immediately.

Rather than continuing to fight, we decided it would likely be better for us to enjoy a tea together. Him in his nightclothes and I dressed as a pauper, we made quite the pair.

"Have you tried this thing they call 'coffee'?" I asked him, trying to get him to talk about the New World somehow. But alas, he was far ahead of me.

Our tea was quite short-lived, as he then brought me down to the Palace's storeroom. It was filled, as he told me, with all sorts of odds and ends that had been gifted to him over the years. I was astonished by all that I saw: bottled beer from England, a mercator projector, and a German printing press.

"Are you using this?" I said, upon seeing the German contraption. I'd been aching to get my hands on one.

"All yours," he said, without even a moment of thought.

I did not know how to express my gratitude to him then, so I continued to peruse the room, looking for other topics of discussion. Luckily, I found a bag of coffee. I weighed it in my hand, smiling.

"I've heard a bit on how to use this," I said, grinning.

"From Arabia," he said, saying the name of the place as though it were a dirty word. My smile seemed to make him nervous.

For the remainder of the night, I made use of that coffee. It was all an elaborate attempt to prove to the King that there are places outside of Spain, outside of Madrid, even, that have many meritorious gifts. I roasted the beans over the fireplace as I'd heard people were supposed to. Then, I ground the beans by hand before pressing them into a small container and pouring boiling water through it. King Phillip watched the whole time, remaining awake with me through the night.

When it was done, I was quite happy with the result. The coffee brought a smile to my face. The King, however, was not so certain.

"Come now," I said, nudging his cup closer to him. "It's only a drink."

Finally, King Phillip raised the cup to his lips and took a sip slowly. There was a pause. Then, to my delight, he took another thoughtful sip.

"It's bitter…and acidic," the King said in his most diplomatic and official voice. "And yet, it's strangely tempting."

He took a large gulp this time, and I followed suit. He let out a sigh of utter contentment. I felt victorious. Then, a thought occurred to him, and he eyed the cup suspiciously.

"But do you think it's Christian?"

We spent the rest of the evening together debating the Catholic merits of many things, coffee being one of them. The most important, however, was the problem of slavery. I spoke my case to the King using the Catholic Bible, lamenting with all the eloquence I could muster. As the hours passed by, Phillip was swayed.

Repartimiento continued in Spanish America and the Philippines, and the Spanish were participatory customers in the African slave trade in the West Indies for a long time. But never again, after that point, would Spain have slave ships under her command.

The following morning, Alice arrives at school early and sits at her desk with the book in her lap. She makes some notes on a pad in front of her: "Seville bakery, Spanish Navy, printing press, mention of imprisonment…M.S."

Her eyes scour the research information she's pulled up on the screen before her. Light from her computer flashes over her face. Hours pass.

Finally, she sits back in her chair, staring at the screen. On it is an online biography of Miguel de Cervantes Saavedra. She picks up Taryn's book in awe. She can hardly believe it.

"I think this is real," she mutters to herself.

She looks at the little pink slip of paper again. Oh, Taryn.

Taryn, at the hospital, excitedly paces before the hospital bed. She's taken this idea of telling the stories of her days as far as she can. It's fun for her.

"So, I caught a train to New York City. I was expelled, y'know, so it didn't matter that I was missing class." She pauses, waiting for her father to respond to this. Normally, he would. When he doesn't, she continues. "I had a run-in with a hooker, but her soul was so clear to me. I wanted to talk to her as a friend I never had. She, however, was better friends with her pimp."

Still no answer. Taryn chuckles a little.

"After experiencing everything the city has to offer during Christmas – yes, they are all still done up this May – my teacher took me in and told me not to wish myself a martyr, but to humbly live what I believe until my last day." She feels her momentum building, so she gets up onto the bed and stands at the foot of it, dramatically towering over her father. "Phoebe wouldn't go west with me, so here I am still. I watched her joyously ride the carousel in the rain. I don't want to say anything else because I miss them all dearly."

With that final flourish, she covers her face as a tragic ending. No response. She peeks through her fingers at her father. She plops down and sits cross-legged.

"Yes, that was the plot of *Catcher in the Rye*. Miss Loureiro is having us each say a monologue for drama. And I was thinking I'd do a one-act adaptation. She said it was spontaneous. And pure-hearted, I think. She said it was generous of me to share my talent. So."

Even though he doesn't respond again, this time Taryn sits down with a smile.

Alice sits at her desk continuing her research after school as well. She still hasn't given the book back to Taryn, but it isn't her fault. It's simply because there's so much incredible research to be done with this text. She can't stop. She knows she's been getting behind on her work because of this, but it's the most interesting thing that's ever happened to her in this school. At this particular moment, her eyes are closed, her hands pressed against the book. She's simply daydreaming about all that could become of it.

When Principal Kelly knocks at the door.

"Yoo-hoo!" he hollers. Alice opens her eyes and hides the book on her lap. "What are you still doing here?"

Alice's eyes flash with frustration, but then she sighs. "Wondering how I came to be on this side of the classroom, I suppose." She thinks of her rejection letter. What a life she's led.

"Nostalgia for youth, eh?" he says as he takes a seat on one of the desks near hers.

"All of us working with kids must have some measure of it, right?" she says. She finds herself unable to stop the wistful tone in her voice. She knows she'll regret it, so she turns the conversation back onto him. "What do you like about kids?"

Kelly takes a long moment to think. "They're easy to manipulate."

Alice looks down, her disgust barely hidden.

Surprisingly, he continues. "Now, now. But for their own good sometimes. You can tell a kid their mom went to a perfect place inside of the facts: her top was on Franklin and her legs were on Federal, guts at the crossroads. Saved me some grief before I was old enough to know what's what."

Alice nods slowly at this, and Kelly looks down to avoid her gaze. She looks down too and is met with the book in her hands.

"They do have imagination," she says. "They're willing to believe. Let something move them because it does and mean something not because someone tells them it's 'supposed to.' It's so hard to catch that again."

Kelly nods. He gets up awkwardly and has to steady the little desk below him. "Maybe we agree on something after all. See you at the benefit."

Alice watches him all the way until he closes the door.

By this point in the night, Taryn is feeling quite bleak. She's run out of most things she knows to talk about. She knows Gloria will be here soon.

"But really, it was kind of like the stage lights on Broadway had been turned on," she says, still talking about her performance. She's been thinking about it all afternoon. "On me, ya know. For the first time. I can't believe they liked the idea, and I didn't throw up or anything."

She takes his hand and sniffs back tears. It's getting harder and harder not to be scared. "I don't know what else to say. I don't have the book, and it's the only thing you seemed to hear. I'll have to get it back somehow. We'll finish it. Maybe Miss Loureiro can help."

She kisses his hand and looks up at the bedside clock. It's almost seven. Her dad would be getting home from work right about now. She sighs deeply.

"Some people think the feelings of isolation go away when the story ends," she muses. "But Salinger went on alone after all the fame…You could be stuck in here alone for a long time but write something that touches the world. Even if it's just in your mind."

She puts her hand on his forehead tenderly. She wishes it would bring him back.

1570

King Phillip and I became fast friends in a way I did not expect. Then, when the Queen passed, I wrote poems to commemorate her. This, I believe, with grateful heart, aided the King in his grief. In doing this, I aided myself in grief as well.

There's some to make

links and chains;

And there's some to make

the chains of love!

For there's steel

to forge and be bent

and there's true love

to find or invent!

So, buy the best metal,

you've money enough,

and join those making

the chains of love!

I was given a seat in the court for these grief-filled poems. Yet, despite them, there was great loss and chaos at sea. The King loved my poetry, but I knew when he deployed troops that my skills would be better served on the battlefield. Experience would feed my writing besides.

I fought bravely, shooting cannons from my ship. I watched enemy vessels sink and saw my men slice their opponents in half. I also had the opportunity to see my dear, brave friend Sir Roderigo again, if for the last time. I wrote to console myself when Roderigo, like a brother to me, my right hand, went down before my eyes. A cannonball came sailing straight towards his ship while his hand reached out to me.

That same day, I found myself faced with a brutally abused bear in chains, wielded by an enemy ship. They tried to release it on my ship with a gangplank, but we wouldn't let them close enough. Then, one of our enemies whipped the bear's backside, and it rushed across their deck and leapt onto mine. He landed right next to me. Before I could react, it lunged at me and mauled my left hand. I felt extreme agony. My right hand dropped my sword, and I placed my intact hand onto the snarling bear's shoulder. The bear was confused but began to calm down very slowly. Together, we rested our heads against one another in the middle of the misery of the war.

After this and the loss of Roderigo, I lost my right hand and had a nub of a left for the rest of my life. But I learned something of human nature and inhuman nature. After witnessing Pope Pius V giving a victory speech to swaths of Italians, Spaniards, and others in 1571, I knew no act of man would ever settle the divides that separate us from God.

I found myself in Tunis in 1574, running from opposing forces with my fellow soldiers. It was a frenzy, every man looking out for himself. I hid behind a huge bale of hay and watched as Don Juan of Austria climbed atop a stack of barrels of wine. He then sliced a rope beneath him, and the barrels tumbled, knocking enemies left and right. Don Juan surfed down the barrels and carved holes into the few men he passed. The wine flowed through the streets, mixing with blood.

"Never too early to celebrate a victory!" he proclaimed.

I admired this man's tactics and drama. I was about to tell him so when I followed his gaze to see an enemy soldier nearly hitting an innocent five-year-old. Don Juan jumped into action before I did. He grabbed hold of the boy and covered him, preparing to die dramatically. The enemy soldier readied his sword to cut through them both.

I couldn't let them die. I grabbed a horse harness and leapt over the six-foot bale of hay I was hiding behind. I wrapped the harness around the soldier's sword like a whip and yanked it out of the soldier's hands.

A peasant mother, clearly the mother of the boy, ran out of a nearby home. She must have witnessed the scene. The boy ran into her arms. I went to help Don Juan to his feet who then ran off in another direction with a wink. I nearly laughed. I was about to follow Don Juan off into the distance when the enemy soldier pulled out another blade and raised it in my direction.

Before I could move, the mother let out a yelp. "Enes! Do you not know your own son?"

Enes stopped and stared between the woman and the child. He remained expressionless. He then pinned my arms behind my back.

"You have saved my son from my own hand," he whispered to me in Turkish. "For that you will live."

And with that, he hauled me off.

The cell they kept me in was dirty and dark, nothing to write home about. I was the only prisoner of that battle. Every other unfortunate Spaniard undertaken was slaughtered. I only wondered of my lord, Don Juan. He may have not only survived but escaped. Or he may have met the end of a sword as soon as he turned the corner from me. But somehow, I imagined he would never die.

When Phillip got around to paying for my release five years later, I had no choice but to return to a life of "freedom." The brilliant sunshine reflecting on the Palacio Real de Madrid blinded me, as did this new free prospect. From then on, my mind was never free of death, of the impossible, of Don Juan, of words, words…

When Alice sees "Don Juan" written in the book, she rubs her thumb over it in amazement. She can't believe it. She's been at the school all night reading, and the answers keep revealing themselves so easily.

"If this is dated pre-1605, there is no denying..." She doesn't even need to finish the sentence for herself. The truth is so apparent, she can hardly believe it.

She opens her rejection email on her computer and starts a new reply. She types: "Dear Princeton Graduate Admissions Committee, I am writing to inform you of a change in my admissions file."

She pulls a mailing envelope from her desk drawer. Within minutes, she's out the door.

When she gets back to her room, Taryn is already there. It's still early. Alice hadn't expected any students for another hour or so.

"Taryn, are you okay?" she says, as the student whirls around to see her instructor entering the room. "Why are you so early?"

Taryn rises, standing perfectly straight. Her expression is very earnest. "Miss Loureiro, my book that Principal Kelly took – remember, you thought it was 'fascinating'?"

Alice nods slowly. She feels something sink in her stomach.

"I realized," Taryn continues. "Maybe you can help me get it back. This is going to sound silly, but please believe me...I've been reading to him. Because well, what else is there to do, and we do that anyway–" She stops herself for a moment. She takes a deep breath. "He moved when I read it to him. And I haven't found anything else that I read or say that has been able to do that. I guess…the odds are worse every day. I need it. Now."

She's crying now, the tears rolling down her face without any sign of stopping. She's embarrassed, but she can't help it. This feels like her last chance.

Alice reaches forward and gently takes Taryn's hand in both of hers. "I got the book back from Principal Kelly."

Taryn can feel relief rushing through her. Everything will be okay.

"But I no longer have it," Alice continues.

All of a sudden, that relief stops. She narrows her eyes.

"I gave it to the most respected institution for the study of Spanish culture and history." Taryn removes her hands, shocked, as Alice continues. The tears become angry ones. "They are going to carbon date it, and there will be handwriting analysis–"

"Why?" Taryn steps back forcefully. "Why would you do that?"

Alice feels desperate now, almost on the edge of tears herself. "Because, Taryn, you and I have made an amazing discovery. I believe Cervantes wrote the book. No original manuscript of Cervantes' published works has been preserved. But the book you, or your father, I suppose, found, was never published. Never before seen! And amazingly well-preserved."

Taryn shakes her head in disbelief. "Who cares? You got to read it. Why do you need the whole world to know?"

"Don't you want to share it?" Alice tries to take Taryn's hands again, but the student won't let her.

"I care about my father. I don't really have room for anything else right now." Taryn's tone is cold. She's emotionally exhausted and shaking so much that she has to look away. Then, she has a thought and whips back to look at Alice. "How does it end?"

"What?"

"Tell me how the book ends. At least I can repeat that to my father."

Alice opens her mouth and then closes it again. Her heart sinks even more. "I didn't finish it."

"What?" The last living part of Taryn's heart breaks.

"I got so excited when it mentioned Don Juan, I just sent it in without reading the rest."

Taryn can't even come up with anything else to say. She closes her eyes and tries to hold back more tears. When she can't, she turns around and leaves.

"We're making history!" Alice calls after her, but it's only halfway enthusiastic. She slouches back in her chair, guilty and upset.

1579

Though Phillip continued to want my assistance in matters that concerned the whole nation, I couldn't handle that anymore. No matter how much he pleaded with me, I couldn't bring myself to join him. I simply looked out the window at Madrid, busy and blanketed by the blue of the sky.

"I only ask for the printing press," I said to the King. "Let me my last solace."

Phillip was saddened by this, but he told his servant to fetch it for me. Once it was set before me, my last desire had been fulfilled.

All through 1580, I wrote. I sat at my desk with a single candle, writing slowly and earnestly. Depression took over. Housemaids brought me my meals, but I didn't eat them often. Even the sound of the door closing when they left was disturbing to me. I began to live very quietly.

In writing, I sought life in death, health in sickness, freedom in prison, escape from entrapment, and loyalty from the traitor. But my fate, from which I've never expected any good to come, joined forces with the heavens above to decree that since I'm asking for the impossible, it won't even give me the possible.

Like the rest of Spain, in 1583, I lost money. My cottage was bare and lonely in the hills of Madrid, but I was content there. One of my few joys came from the distribution of my poems to some select friends abroad. The Spaniards were different, downtrodden and ignorant. Even those few foreign admirers were far more than I had in Madrid.

I especially enjoyed encouraging younger unknown writers experimenting with forms the world could use reinvigorated. I once received one such letter from a friend, reading, "From fairest creatures we desire increase, That thereby beauty's rose might never die..."

I responded quickly: "Dear Will, might this not prove the beginnings of a story for the stage?"

I could not make a living writing for myself and friends, however. I got another job back with the Navy as a commissioner. It was tedious work for someone with an eye for detail, not for someone with big ideas. While staring down tax forms in the late evening hours, I hesitated at my quill. Could we not find a simpler way to make sure we paid the taxes we owed?

The clerks I worked with never had an ear for these kinds of questions. They would just snappily drop another stack of papers on my desk, lifting a cloud of dust. "Your job is to follow instructions and stay in line like any good officer," they would say. "If you don't want to do it, someone else will."

But I still had big ideas. While the clerks were polishing the buttons of Superior Officers, I wrote on fresh pieces of paper that I hid between piles. When I looked out the window, I could see myself at five, skipping through a similar countryside, laughing, dancing in the grass. It was always a bittersweet memory.

I wanted to spend my life looking for opportunities to do something, everything, to help my fellow Spaniard and the world. And I wanted to be admired. My heart was clearly not in this work. I saved for many months until I was freed from poverty. I became much better at following instructions, looking forward to the day I would be my own master again, captain of my own ship. The stacks of work diminished. The only writing I cared about was not that of the Navy but my own.

One day, in 1590, I quit.

"Ah, Officer del Canto," the Superior Officer said. "Just the man I wanted to see."

His face showed quite the opposite emotion, and his stern expression terrified me. The clerk, next to him, had a smug smile. He held up an old tax form of mine, one from when I had only just started this post. One from before I began to write, when I didn't understand this work as simply a means to an end.

I was arrested in front of the whole office. I did my best to protest. No one listened to me. No one cared that I knew the King. I *offered to pay for the mistake out of my own pocket, but the clerk just smiled smugly and sat back in his chair.*

I was thrown into another cell. It too was damp and dark and horrible. Of course, no one thought to actually bother the King to see if he really did know a lowly naval commissioner with no family and modest savings, a "tax evader" by careless error and a spiteful subordinate. I wished I had given my clerk a nicer Christmas gift, perhaps one of my famous ensaimadas. The food in prison was nowhere close to that delicious. But deeper down, I knew there was nothing I could have done to please him but get out of his way.

Without a window to the world, I decided to make my own. I had a single sheet of paper in my pocket. I leaned out of my cell and spoke to the guard, who I would later learn was named Silvestre.

"Excuse me, good sir," I called. The guard turned to me with suspicion. I realized, after a moment, that he wouldn't be verbally responding to me at all. "I may not seem like much at the moment. I apologize for my compromised appearance. But I believe I am one of Spain's finest people. I have a fine wit and imagination, and I want to share with you a quick drama, to spread to a fellow Spaniard the joys of a little theater."

Silvestre didn't respond then either, but he seemed dumbfounded. I was happy to have gained my audience's attention.

"All right then, splendid. There is, however, a slight catch. I would like a little exchange. A quill and ink for opening night. A sheet of paper for every night after."

Silvestre considered this. "I need to see if you are any good first."

"Fair enough," I said with a grin. I paused a moment to get into character and then stepped against the bars once more, giving the most exquisite acting performance I possibly could. "What light through yonder window breaks! It is the east, and Juliet is the sun!"

I could see Sil's expression cracking just slightly, so I continued, pushing it over the edge. I grabbed some hay from the floor of my cell and quickly fashioned a long blonde wig. "Romeo," I continued. "Romeo. Wherefore art thou, Romeo?"

"Stop!" Sil begins to laugh so hard he can hardly control himself. He wipes tears of laughter from his face.

"I'm glad you were entertained," I said, trying to further convince him of my side if he wasn't fully already. "It's not really a comedy, but — It really is the best up-and-coming talent. My friend Will in London is working on it. I told him he's struck gold and to keep at it, don't you think?"

Sil nodded slowly. "I think the deal is fair," he said with hesitance. "But no one can know I am giving you anything, understand? Can I trust you?"

I let my straw wig fall apart onto the floor around me. "You have my word. The King's seal is behind it."

Sil's eyes went big at that. "You? If you're a friend of the King, why are you in here?"

I grin, the first real I've felt in weeks. "I'm just taking some time to write."

Sil nodded slowly, a smile of his own growing on his face. We shook hands through the bars.

Sil was good on his promise, and I immediately began a new journey, looking into myself instead of out to the wide world beyond the prison walls. Each day, Sil snuck me a new sheet of paper that I'd add to the top of my small stack. My hair grew longer with time, and my eyes grew more hopeful. I was pioneering a new literary form. In the darkest hold of Spain, at a time far from what felt to me the golden age of my mother country, I decided to write the tale of my own life. You are reading my story, but it is a story after all. I have made myself a character. Fortunately, there is no expense but time to fear, wandering lost in the La Mancha of my mind. There is no window out. This is the window into my world.

I call it the "novel."

At Princeton University, entire states away from Taryn and Alice's troubles, Daylet Dominguez is having a late night in his office. He hasn't been home since receiving the manuscript from a Miss Alice Loureiro from Boston. Now, after hours and hours of reading, he looks up from the book with extreme shock, discovery, and then excitement.

He looks to his TA who is fast asleep in the otherwise empty office.

"Tim!" The TA wakes with a start. "Get me a meeting with Dean Schwartz tomorrow, ASAP. And the President!"

Tim stares at him groggily. "What?"

"Of the school. Though the White House should know too. History is in my hands!"

Tim stares at the book in Daylet's hands.

Alice sluggishly peruses the aisles of colored pencils and smiling cartoon "progress chart" characters. Another day gathering classroom supplies. She picks up a sticker sheet of gold stars that say, "You're a Star!"

She looks at it, a bit dubious. Then, she puts it back and chooses a mildly excited line of zoo animals, a zebra with a flag that says, "Even the last gets a chance!"

Another teacher shuffles by, one who looks much older than Alice, and muses to herself as she looks at the stickers. "The best way to spend a Saturday!"

Alice shakes her head at this, a bit disgusted. How did her life get to this point? As she turns into a new aisle, her cell begins to ring from an unknown number.

"Hello?" she says as she accepts the call.

"Alice Loureiro?"

"Yes?"

"This is Professor Dominguez at Princeton."

Alice almost laughs out of shock. "Oh!"

"We are so excited about the book and its origin possibilities! We are organizing a conference with the Dean of the department at our partner campus at the University of

Seville right now. We'd like you to discuss with us the possibility that this was indeed the first modern novel, written by Miguel Cervantes."

Alice silently jumps up and down in the aisle. "Yes!"

"Excellent," he says, and she can hear paper shuffling on the other end of the line. "And you are on our grad program waitlist, correct?"

"Yes, I am," she says, nearly breathless.

"Well, our admissions board is as excited about this as we are. The book is just–"

"Wait," she says, remembering Taryn and her father. "Is it possible for me to have more time with the book before the hearing?"

There's a pause on the line.

"Oh," Daylet says. "Well, it's in Seville undergoing carbon dating and handwriting analysis. I didn't realize you hadn't extensively analyzed it…"

"I was just so excited…"

Another silence on the line.

"Best not let the board know that," he says slowly. "I am excited about this as well, and from what I read, I believe it. I know the labs in Seville are finishing tonight, and the results will be delivered at the hearing Monday morning. If you can get to Seville, before Monday morning, you can look at the book."

Alice looks down at her cart full of school supplies. She makes a decision to leave it behind and walks out the double doors of the store.

"I can do that."

She runs straight to her classroom first. She grabs her laptop from the desk and curls up under her desk to grab her charging cord. She struggles to unplug it as she scrolls through flights on her phone in her other hand. Every flight for the night is full. There's only one seat left for Sunday night. It's first class, priced at two grand.

Alice grimaces. She pulls up her banking app. She has a little under two grand in her checking account.

She runs through the halls with her laptop in her arms. When she makes it to Principal Kelly's office, Ms. Scarry is there, filing her nails. She embarrassedly puts down the filer and starts typing randomly to look busy when Alice arrives.

"Is Principal Kelly in?"

"He's out," Miss Scarry replies shortly.

"When will he be back?"

The phone rings. Miss Scarry answers. Alice glares at her.

"It's fine. I'll run into him on my way out," she says and turns around, leaving the lazy secretary in her wake.

On her way out the door, she glances at the last available seat on her phone once again. Against her better judgment, she presses the "purchase" button.

Alice jogs straight to the parking lot. She rounds a corner of the school building and quite literally runs into Principal Kelly, causing him to drop the red apple he's munching on. He looks down at it angrily and slowly stoops to retrieve it.

"I'm…I'm sorry," Alice says hurriedly. "I need to talk to you."

"Apple?" he says with a snarky tone, gesturing with the apple now in his hand.

"Only green for me," she says with a frown.

"I was actually about to call you."

Alice stops in her tracks. She's confused. "Why?"

"For a time to pick you up for tonight," he says. Her heart sinks.

"Tonight?

"The benefit."

"Oh." Her mind spins through every way she can apologize her way out of this.

"I thought we might actually have a fun time," he says, reading her tone entirely wrong. "It's for the school–"

"I'm for the school, and I'm sorry, but I have to fly to Spain. I just need an advance to buy the ticket." She's rushing through her words, providing no explanation in the slightest.

"Is there…a Spanish guy?" He looks strangely crestfallen, and Alice is insulted by the mere thought of it.

"No! I…" She looks down at her hands and then back up at him. She has to lead with confidence. "I am going to a conference with the Princeton board about Cervantes. He wrote that book you confiscated from Taryn. It's actually the first modern novel ever written! I think."

He does not give her the reaction she's hoping for. "Who's Cervantes?"

"The author of *Don Quixote*," she says with a sigh. "Did you even go to school?"

Kelly turns red at this, clearly reading the insult. "You don't have to prove anything to stuck-up literature elitists who didn't want you in the first place."

"I was wait-listed!" she almost-yells it, and it echoes through the parking lot. "That means 'maybe' they want me! And now they definitely will, because I made the biggest literary discovery since Anne Frank's diary!"

"Which was written by a little girl," Kelly says. "I thought you would give the book back to Taryn. Fantasy is a child's game, Alice. We've all got to grow up."

With that, he munches on his dirty apple. Alice watches, almost feeling sorry for him.

"So, about the advance and getting Monday off…"

"If you don't come in Monday, you'll lose your job."

Alice is struck by the finality of his statement. She opens and closes her mouth, searching for something to say. "Just because you're angry I'm not interested in you?"

"Because you're only interested in yourself." He fumbles in his pocket and pulls out a green apple. "I already knew you like green."

He tosses it at her playfully, but she lets it fall to the ground. She looks at him for a moment, seemingly thinking through something, and then walks right past toward the parking lot. Kelly watches her go.

"Hey!" he yells after her, gesturing to the window over his left shoulder. "Is this your classroom?"

Alice doesn't look back. "It was."

Kelly juggles the apple and pitches it as hard as he can into the window. It thuds and plops to the ground, leaving barely a mark. He looks at the window for a second, his shoulders sagging, and uses his elbow to clean the smudge.

As Alice makes it through airport security, she pulls up the airline app. Boarding in thirty minutes. She races toward the gate.

She gets an alert on her phone and she slows to a brisk walk to check it. $5000 was just deposited into her bank account and a text immediately follows from Kelly, "Call it a first-class severance package. No strings attached. Good luck."

The journey is long. Her plane and the sun sweep past each other over the Atlantic Ocean. The world spins as the plane nears Europe, then Spain, before darkness swaths all, and the twinkling lights of Madrid appear. When Alice arrives, she finds herself catching her breath before the Palacio Real de Madrid, exactly the same as it was 500 years ago. She boards a night train with the diverse group characteristic of that type of transportation: Australian tourists, American students, and elderly Spanish citizens touting souvenirs from the capital.

When she arrives in the Seville countryside, the sun rises, as if acknowledging her arrival. The University's building lies behind an eighteenth-century facade of a Royal tobacco factory.

All is quiet in the stunning lobby when Alice arrives. It's barely past 6 AM. There's a single open office door a bit to her right, so she decides to check inside that room first. She opens the door even more. It squeaks loudly.

A young man fumbles awake from behind the President of the University's desk. He quickly stands.

"Hey. You must be Alice," he says with a grin. "I'm American too, so I'm like your ambassador. From Princeton."

She's taken aback by his grin and holds out her hand. "Oh, Professor Daylet!"

"Well, no," he says with a slight grimace. "I'm Professor Daylet's TA."

He shakes her hand anyway. She shakes it and waits. He rubs his eyes, taking a long pause to fall asleep on his feet before responding.

"Oh!" He goes to grab a carefully wrapped package off the desk and hands it to her with a slight bow. Alice tries hard not to laugh.

"Thank you," she says, noting his awkward stance.

"I was keeping it until you arrived. And with that, I'll see you at the conference! 9 AM!"

The door clicks shut. There is silence.

She takes a moment to simply be still. She looks up at the buttresses of the incredible building and lightly feels the book in front of her. She pulls out her extensive notes and research and then unwraps the package. Daylet has packed piles of detailed notes with it as well.

She sets hers aside and then skims his. What a surreal moment.

She opens the book to where she left off.

1596

Phillip had let the coffers ache for hunger again. Food in prison was scarce, and even paper was rare everywhere else. I'd finish my performances in my barely lit cell and receive my few scraps of paper from Sil each time. Yet, now, he seemed more ashamed than he had before as he turned away into the shadows.

I sharpened my quill with my teeth and arranged each scrap so that I could write. While I did my work, I often wondered of that ingenious gentleman of lowly birth, my lord in battle, the chivalrous knight suspended in our modern age, Don Juan. That is, until one day when the perpetually dark cell next to mine began to rustle.

"Who's there?" I called.

I was met with a loud yawn. Don Juan emerged from a pile of hay and into the slight light given from the torch before my cell.

"Don Juan!" I was shocked. "I wondered if you might have met your fate in Tunis! Or if you had climbed your way to the stars!"

Don Juan graciously bowed his head then. "The young, brave Benito. Have you a drink?"

"No, afraid not, sir. We are imprisoned after all."

"Oh," he said, as though just realizing. "Yes."

"Have you been here this whole many years? I never noticed your arrival!"

"Oh, I've been here forever, I think," he said, grinning. "I've merely been asleep."

"You have quite the propensity for sleep," I said, still in disbelief at his being there at all.

"There's only one thing bad about sleep," he declared. "That it resembles death. There's very little difference between a sleeping man and a corpse."

I nodded. "Until death, it is all life, Don Juan."

"Is it better?" he asked me. "All I know is that, while I'm asleep, I'm never afraid. I have no hopes, no struggles, no glories — and bless the man who invented sleep, a cloak over all human thought. And universal currency with which all things can be bought, weight and balance that brings the shepherd and the king, the fool and the wise, to the same level."

"All of Spain is in the same pit of debt, it's true," I mused with a sigh. This was met with a sad silence shared by the two of us. I tried as I could to change the subject. "How did you come to be thrown in prison, then?"

"Antwerp."

Antwerp was the center of the entire international economy. Hundreds of ships per day. The streets were literally paved with gold, and the ships only brought pepper and cinnamon. Phillip was earning seven times the gold in those ports than in the New World. But my little Seville did well, sending American silver there before Phillip was in the hole again in '57.

That is, until the Protestants rebelled, and this bloody war began. Don Juan led his Tercio to Antwerp in '74, after training new volunteers with the foremost military tactics. We lost many of our official men at Tunis but saved many innocents.

Our troops were the best in the world. Fighting cowardly bankers was no problem for Don Juan and his men. The troops ransacked international trading houses, turning fat Venetian bankers to the hysterical streets. The money became the problem. Don Juan's men were of honor, but after years without sufficient pay from the Crown, they took what they believed was theirs, forever ruining the golden city. Don Juan watched it all from atop a hill, tied to a post.

"Mutiny," I said.

Don Juan nodded slowly. "Except for you, Benito."

"Me?" I narrowed my eyes, confused. "No, I was in a Turkish prison for five years, Don Juan."

"Were you?"

Don Juan began to spin a tale that began with a deafening growl that echoed across the pastures and fields.

"You know the legend of Antwerp," Don Juan continued. "Antigoon, the giant under the bridge. He demanded payment to cross. That's how my volunteer men easily entered the golden gates."

"But you had no gold to pay," I said.

"Yes, Benito." He lightly gestured to my hand. "If you have no gold, Antigoon will take a hand and throw it into the river Scheldt. Thank you for your sacrifice."

I took a step back. "I lost my hand to a great bear in the Battle of Lepanto."

"A great bear?" Don Juan chuckled as though the idea was entirely absurd. "No, without you, my troops would have never entered Antwerp. Antwerp would never have fallen. It was an important and terrible victory for Spain. You gave everything for Spain, Benito. That is an honor."

"To strip the crossroads of our modern world of its children, gold, and promise?" I spoke softly. It had been so long since I had spoken to another like this. "Is that honor?"

"The wounds received in battle bestow honor. They do not take it away."

"This lonely spot of moon upon the Earth was not burned out of honor. The best that can be said is it was scorched out of love. Honor is pure, love is war."

I thought back to that day, the Battle of Lepanto. What a strange violence it had been. I thought back to resting my head against that of the great bear as the waves thrashed and explosions faded to peace.

"Well," Don Juan said, clearing his throat and bringing me back to reality. *"Which story do you believe is the truth?"*

"I think I'd rather believe neither if I hadn't only a phantom hand." I tried as I could to make it a joke, but it didn't sound like one.

"The truth may be stretched thin, but it never breaks, and it always surfaces above lies, as oil floats on water. Destiny guides our fortunes more favorably than we could have expected. Look here, Benito, my friend, and see there are wild giants, and with whom I intend to do battle and kill each and all of them so with their stolen booty we can begin to enrich ourselves. This is noble, righteous warfare."

"There is no righteous warfare," I said simply. I closed my eyes, transporting myself away to somewhere where windmills turned to giants. *"What giants?"*

"The ones you can see in your dreams with the huge arms, some of which are nearly two leagues long."

I chuckled. *"Now look, what I see aren't giants but windmills. What seem to be arms are just their sails that go around in the window!"*

Don Juan laughed at that, so high-pitched it sounded like a battle cry. *"Obviously, you don't know much about adventures."*

Later that night, I wrote down the whole conversation Don Juan and I had. I couldn't believe my luck. When I finished transcribing,

I found myself bored once again. I moved to the edge of my cell once more.

"Don Juan?" I called once but to no avail. I tried again. "Don Juan!"

After a slight rustle, Don Juan's nose peeked out.

"I think, finally, from so little sleeping and so much writing, my brain has dried up, and I've gone completely out of my mind!" I whispered loudly enough for him to hear even in the darkness.

"When life itself seems lunatic, who knows where madness lies?" Don Juan grinned, knowing the brilliance of his words. "Perhaps to be too practical is madness. To surrender dreams – that's maybe madness. Too much sanity may be madness and maddest of all; to see life as it is, and not as it should be! Write that down."

I couldn't keep myself from smiling as I scrawled down his words as fast as I could. Before I could finish writing, Don Juan was gone, and Sil rattled my cell. I stood, ready for my performance.

"Come," I began. "Let's away to prison: We two alone will sing like birds in the cage."

"This is a good one," I heard Sil reassuring someone. No matter. However large my audience, I'd give the same show.

"As if we were God's spies: and we'll wear out in a walled prison, packs and sects of great ones, that ebb and flow by the moon."

Sil turned and bowed to someone. "A little something from the don's friend in the Northern Isles."

Before I knew what to think of his comment, King Phillip II entered the little circle of light, clapping. "My, it is dark," he declared. "If I could see you better, Benito, I'm sure you would look awful."

I felt my mouth go dry at his presence. I'd entirely given up hope that this day would come. "Phillip. It has been long."

"I'm here to let you out, friend," he said slowly. "I'm sorry I did not come sooner this time."

"It was not so quick last time."

Phillip frowned with guilt at this. I tried hard not to let my emotions show even though they threatened to bubble over for the first time in my life.

"You did evade taxes, Benito," he said. "That is some form of stealing from the Crown. From Spain."

"I have given everything for Spain." I spoke persuasively and strongly. "And I am not sure if it was right. But I would do it again. Not with a sword, but with a pen. You must put down the sword too, Phillip."

"I don't fight anything but death at my age, Benito."

"I mean your armies and Armada." I remembered my time in the New World. I remembered Roderigo. "This war will go on for eighty years! You fight on so many fronts. It's tearing Spain apart at the pocket seams."

"There are many rebellions and evil attackers," the King said, shaking his head. "Did you not see their vices? It is our responsibility to keep the world right."

"It is not Spain's responsibility to discover whether the afflicted, the enchained, and the oppressed whom she encounters are reduced to these circumstances and suffer this distress for their vices, or for their virtues: her sole responsibility is to secure them as people in need, having eyes only for their sufferings, not for their misdeeds."

"You are a poet, Benito," he said, making that concession. Still, he shook his head. "I like that about you, but it is not just."

"Your search for justice will have no end and bring much suffering. Neither good nor evil can last forever. It follows that as evil has lasted a long time, good must now be close at hand."

I stuck my one hand and my one nub through the bars. Phillip laughed and shook my nub good-naturedly. Then, after a gesture to Sil, they took off my chains. I bowed to Phillip in gratitude, despite our disagreements.

"Come, friend." The King held out a hand to me. "A bath is long overdue."

"I will meet you at the palace, my lord. I must gather my things."

The King looked over my shoulder at my cell behind me. "Do you have gold hidden in the hay?"

Both of us chuckled.

"Perhaps," I said. The fact of the matter was that I didn't know then if it was truly gold or not.

When Phillip left, I went back into my cell. I immediately found myself confused. I couldn't find the papers. I frantically rummaged in the hay until I froze in realization.

I was not the only one in the drama. Don Juan was not the only other player. The most perceptive character in the play is the fool because the man who wishes to seem simple cannot possibly be a simpleton. Sil had stolen my papers, perhaps realizing they could be published for some amount of money. And Phillip was right. I had nothing but moldy memories imprisoned in my mind.

I found myself in deep despair.

Alice stares at the writing with amazed confusion. She's only got about a sixth of the book left to read. She closes it once more and looks at the cover. How incredible.

Then, as if on cue, the door to the office swings open. Alice, startled, looks up at the clock: just seconds from 9:00. Daylet enters with a genuinely thrilled smile.

"Here we go," he says, by way of introduction.

"But…" Alice stands, immediately lost in thought. "He writes that the novel he spent years writing was stolen! What, then, is this? I must finish it!"

She holds up the book in concern. Daylet looks nervous but not particularly surprised. He reaches for her hand and leads her out of the office and across the lobby to the door of the lecture hall. The huge doors open before her. Alice tries hard not to think about the intense looks Daylet keeps giving her, as if to tell her to finish the rest of the book immediately.

When she enters the hall, she finds a gorgeous, centuries-old open space, filled with world-class scholars. A couple key members sit in chairs on the floor in the front row. These include the Rectorate of the University of Seville, Princeton's Dean of Spanish History, and the Chairman of the Board of Graduate Admissions for Princeton. They each sport nameplates. It all resembles a courtroom. In the middle of the floor is a table and chair with a paper nameplate for her.

Daylet gestures to it kindly and takes a seat in the corner. Alice's heart is racing. She's trying her best to keep calm. She sits in her seat and lays the book on the table before her.

She settles in just as the program begins.

"We don't normally hold such a convening of minds in a physical setting such as this to discuss important possible discoveries of interest to the many scholarly fields represented here." The Rectorate's voice is leveled and deep. "We make arguments in our respective journals, and if we're feeling very saucy, we involve the media."

He smiles with a twinkle in his eye, and most of the audience members crack a smile or give a light chuckle.

"After what happened with Harvard and the 'Gospel of Jesus' Wife,' we like to chemically date the paper and ink before publicly announcing the possibility of a discovery of this importance to the international literary community, and of course to Spain herself. It's also better if the individual responsible for turning our attention to the artifact discloses their identity. Anonymity can come off a bit suspect to the public."

He and everyone else then looks towards Alice expectantly. She notices a transcriber in the corner, taking notes on everything said. With all these eyes on her, her confidence falters.

"Um, yes–"

"Hold on." The Rectorate holds up a hand. "Please speak into the microphone."

She realizes then that there is a microphone at the corner of the desk. She pulls it toward her and addresses the room.

"My name is Alice Loureiro. I teach 7th and 8th grade Spanish at Adams Upper Public School in Boston, MA." She scans the room in between words. With each sentence, she gets slightly more comfortable hearing her voice bouncing back at her through the speakers. "I sent the book to Professor Daylet Dominguez with the opinion it is an authentic fictionalized autobiography by Miguel de Cervantes."

The Rectorate clears his throat. "You are the owner of the book?"

There is a tense beat. Alice looks at the waiting crowd and then at the book in front of her.

"No," she says truthfully. "The owner is my student, twelve-year-old Tayrn Michaels."

The transcriber types this.

The Rectorate nods. "Very well. I understand you are a candidate for admission into our affiliate institution, Princeton's Graduate program in Spanish History. The Golden Age Literary Program held here on our campus, specifically."

"Yes." Alice nearly jumps out of her seat when her admission is brought up.

"That is why we are here today, as the Chairman of the Board of Graduate Admissions and the Dean of Spanish History have a special interest in a real-time discussion."

The Dean begins to speak, taking the cue from the Rectorate. "This 'novel' provides a reason to reconsider what we thought we knew about perhaps the most influential author of all time, Miguel Cervantes. The line between his life and writings is blurred by the introduction of this possible autobiography, predating *Don Quixote*."

"Very well," the Rectorate says. "Let's begin the presentation of the evidence."

Over the next couple of hours, various scholars and scientists present speeches on the book. Alice is amazed over and over again at the in-depth nature of their research, considering that the book had only been discovered recently. She finds herself stunned by the testing of paper and carbon ink, the carbon dating of materials, and the handwriting peculiarities unique to Cervantes.

During the conclusion of one particular gloved scientist holding up a sample of the paper of the book, an impossibly old paleographer stands up in the crowd. He speaks much more loudly than his frail form will suggest. No one dares interrupt this possibly senile man, most definitely not Alice.

"The rules for deciphering the old handwritings that one encounters in documents of an earlier date than that of the seventeenth century are embodied in two distinct though related and interacting sciences. The first of these is the science of Paleography, which has for its province the mere deciphering of the writings, as well as questions concerning the nature of the material upon which it is imposed, of the implements by which it was produced and of the medium through which recorded. Diplomatic, the second of the sciences, is chiefly concerned with the style, the peculiar formulas which kept changing from age to age, the special methods of assigning dates, and even the individuals who produced them. 'Paleography studies the body, while Diplomatic studies the soul of the document.' Let's get to discussing the soul of the document. Even if this is Cervantes', the details of the story are too preposterous to validate."

The old man moves to take a seat, very slowly. The entire room's eyes remain on him. There's a beat of silence after he's entirely out of view.

"All's well that ends well," the Chairman says, drawing attention for the first time today. "May I interrupt, Rectorate?"

"Yes, of course," he says, leaning back from his microphone. "Ms. Martyn, chairman of the Board of Admissions at Princeton."

"I would like to hear Ms. Loureiro's opinion on the ending of the book. Did he know the ending before he started writing?" There's a beat of silence. "How does it all make sense?"

Alice gulps. Her hands begin to shake. She opens her mouth to speak.

"Well…"

1600

I found myself in Istanbul, gliding through its stunning architecture, Turkish rugs, and playful music. I greeted children who laughed and clapped when I arrived. I was known by all as the storyteller, the one who would always tell a good tale.

I spoke in Turkish, telling new stories left and right. I remember the local favorite, that of Quixu. "He was a grand merchant," I would say. "And he was stranded in the desert with only his camel for a friend. But lo and behold, after three days of searching, an oasis sprang forth from the sand."

At that, I'd make a small puddle bubble up from the ground. Children would shriek and clap. This put me in the perfect position to continue: "Now, our foolish hero took to the sea..."

In 1603, I journeyed to England to meet up with my good friend Will who premiered his shows at the Globe Theater. He allowed me the great honor of performing as "Gertrude" in his play,

Hamlet. Shakespeare, too, would prepare to perform, but he was always frantic at the last minute. We'd apply our lipstick together in the mirror.

"The play's the thing wherein I'll catch the conscience of the king," he'd say to me in the dressing room often. "I simply wish to sleep."

I'd pat him gently on his arm and say, "I knew another man who relished a sleep to end the heartache. 'Tis a consumption devoutly to be wished. To die, to sleep — to sleep, perchance to dream. Ay, therein lies the rub; for in that sleep of death what dreams may come? Best stick with the dreams you already know. Your play, Will."

Will would always then whip out his script and quill. "But should the inflection be here or there?!"

I'd reach across and lower the quill. Will always got caught up in the details.

"A comma does not a play make. Punctuation is not the question. This play — will it be? To be or not to be — that is the question."

"You are magic, Miguel!" Will said that time. "Magic!"

I did no more than powder my nose with a smile.

One night, in 1605, I found myself walking along an old path in Seville beneath the stars. I noticed a small boy, nearly six years old, who appeared over the next hill and began to walk towards me. I passed the boy, thinking nothing of him, until something compelled me to turn around.

"Have you ever seen snow?" I called after him.

"Snow?" the boy said, confused.

I gestured for the boy to come closer. "When I was a boy, at exactly one hour, eleven minutes prior to the sun's appearance in the eastern sky, something magnificent happened. Out of the clear sky, large white saucers began to descend to the earth, as peaceful as anything I had ever witnessed."

I pointed up to the dark sky, and the boy looked up too. A single white speck slowly descended from high in the star-filled sky. As it neared, it grew larger and larger. I reached out to catch it, a snowflake as large as a plate. I held it before the boy's eyes, watching them grow wide.

"Do you know how to read?" I asked him.

The boy shook his head. I held up my nub with a gentle smile.

"My magic wand," I said to him. I waved my nub over the snowflake, and it dissipated into a thousand little snowflakes, swept up in the breeze, revealing my book, this book in my palm. "You will learn," I said.

I offered the book to the boy. He took it cautiously and then pulled it close to his chest. As he ran off down the road, I smiled up at the sky.

"Benito spent the rest of his life traveling the world telling stories that helped people. Stories that were truly magical. Everyone who heard them became hopeful and optimistic."

With that, Taryn looks up from her handwritten notebook. Her dad breathes quietly, still unconscious. She looks out to

Boston, all the parts of the city she can see outside the hospital window.

She sighs. Nothing has changed.

In the lecture hall, Alice breathes slowly. She scans the room, filled with expectant scholars. Her chest hurts with nerves. Even though this is what she's wanted for so long, she can't handle actually being here. Everything depends on this moment.

"Well…" she begins, releasing her breath, releasing all the wasted years of her life. Letting the light in.

In a dream I have, Don Juan lunges at the giants. The sky is gray and swirled, strange like a fantasy. The wind howls, and I squint to see Don Juan in the midst of action.

"Don Juan!" I holler.

Don Juan cuts off a giant's arm. The giant slows down into slow motion. All the giants start to stiffen.

"Don Juan!"

The giants fade back into huge windmills. Don Juan freezes, in my dream, mid-fight.

"You are tilting at windmills!"

The wind dies down. Don Juan pants a little and lowers his sword. He turns to Benito.

"I am tilting at the windmills?" Don Juan hollers as he approaches me with his wide strides. The sky begins to brighten around him into a more typical sunny day. "No, Miguel, it is you

who loves to dream what you do not know, to fight the imaginary foe."

In this dream, I sit in the grass and close my eyes. Don Juan sits alongside me.

"I'm so tired," I say simply. I lean back in the grass and close my eyes.

"Why do you want so badly to return to the prison of your mind? Do you feel safe there in the dark? You have escaped into a fantasy, in a fantasy you at least are willing to admit you control."

I open one eye and stare at Don Juan suspiciously. Don Juan turns to the sun and smiles under the warm rays. The grass becomes sand beneath them, and the sound of waves gives way to the full beach.

"You are not mad, Miguel," Don Juan says with a smile. "You are dreaming. To surrender dreams – this may be madness. Too much sanity may be madness and maddest of all: to see life as it is and not as it should be! Wake up, Miguel."

Somewhere far away, Peter sees a man. It is 1605. He cannot feel his body, but he can feel his consciousness for the first time in god-knows how long. A man, who he recognizes as Miguel de Cervantes from a middle school project he'd done with his friends, writes in a book: "Don Juan."

The man crosses out "Juan" and writes "Quixote."

The man looks up as if in a trance and glances out his pleasant little window, overlooking Seville. He rubs his temple. He takes a sip of water from a glass.

"Wake up," the man says to himself. Peter feels the words echoing through his body too, as though he were the one speaking. Then, Miguel looks Peter in the eyes.

"Wake up," he says again, gently. He moves to set down the water glass.

In the Boston hospital room, far away from Peter's actual consciousness, a water glass is set by his bedside.

All of the eyes of the distinguished audience members are on Alice. She swallows, hard.

"Well, I...I didn't quite finish the book," she admits. "I only got–"

Tim shuffles over to her then with a glass of water. The microphone blasts feedback. While the room recovers, he whispers to her.

"Open to the end."

Alice fumbles with the book. Right past where she left off, the pages are blank. The entire rest of the book is nothing. She flips to the last page she read. It is truly the last line, but on the back of the page, there is a sketch of a beautiful cathedral bell tower. *My home of Seville, April 22, 1616.*

"The day Cervantes died," she whispers after a shocked gasp. "The day before Shakespeare died."

The Rectorate clears his throat, urging her to speak up. Alice clears her throat in return.

"If he knew he would die that day, he knew this would be the last of his writing." Her confidence is clear in her voice, clearer than it's ever been. "Perhaps the pages he wrote in prison were found, the guard had sold them, and they turned up. Perhaps this was the first modern novel, before *Don Quixote*. But why date it the day of his death, years later?"

A stuffy professor stands. "To answer the Chairman's question, none of it is true. We already know Cervantes was one of seven children of a pharmacist, a simple soldier turned rather unsuccessful playwright. He was in and out of prison for financial reasons. He was excommunicated from the cathedral across the street! Why spin romantic tales of a man who was clearly a hero nowhere but on the page! Call this a pure fiction warm-up to *Don Quixote*, if you can even find the evidence to prove Cervantes wrote it."

Alice looks at the careful, delicate sketch of the cathedral bell tower in the book. She stands. "Perhaps after his factual autobiography was stolen, years later when he knew he was at the end of his life, he decided to write it all again. He decided to correct his mistakes on paper. After *Don Quixote* was a success, he wrote himself a fictional autobiography."

"What does that even–"

The Rectorate holds up a hand to silence the professor. He gestures for Alice to continue.

"But this time," she says, a smile growing on her face. "He wrote it the way he experienced it, from a perspective of hope and love for his country. The life that he created in his mind, one of incredible imagination and nearly insurmountable circumstance. A lonely life full of heartaches but comforted by the power of a pen and an undying desire to share the joy of literature with the world."

The transcriber lets out a gleeful yelp as she types up the juicy speech. She's embarrassed when she realizes everyone is looking at her. She looks at her clock.

"The time is up," she declares.

"If anyone here of proper standing with an academic journal wishes to pursue this topic with a peer-reviewed paper, I'm sure we'd all be interested." The Rectorate pushes his glasses back up his nose. "Ms. Loureiro, I trust you will return the artifact to its rightful owner?"

Alice nods, thinking once again of Taryn. She tries not to appear too shaken.

"All are dismissed. Thank you."

The reception is in full swing shortly afterwards. Older scholars snack on refreshments of wine and cheese. Alice glances at a few who clearly avert their eyes. No one is willing to speak with her. She spies a stairwell corridor and slips away. No need to mingle. It's been a long few days.

Alice reaches the top stair, wipes away a tear, and takes in the dusty attic space. A huge, decorative window lets in light. She can see she's looking out the front facade. Across the street is the cathedral drawn in the book. She spends a moment taking in the incredibly history around her.

She sits on a beam. Her phone vibrates. Surprised, she reads a text from Principal Kelly: "How'd it go?"

Alice sighs, bothered, and puts it away. She hears a creak behind her. To her even greater surprise, Professor Daylet Dominguez navigates his way to her beam.

"Do you mind?" he asks, already apologetic.

She gestures that he's welcome, not wanting to make a fool of herself anymore.

"Tim pointed me up here," he says once he sits down next to her. "I understand, those receptions are no fun. Everybody just talks about themselves and how world-changing their latest research will be and compares grants."

They look out the window together at the sunlight over the ancient street. Alice strokes the book in her lap, almost protectively.

"I thought this was a window to Cervantes we had never before had," she says with a dry chuckle. "On this other planet we live on, where people can bother you from around the world."

Daylet laughs lightly too.

"I'm just sorry I wasted your time," she finished with a sigh.

"It's literature. It's foremost a window to ourselves. And I'm glad it was also our window from Princeton to you, a brave and bright inquisitor."

"Dreamer." She rolls her eyes.

"We want people with a sense of adventure in our program. Otherwise–" He offers his hand for the book. "I need that prop to deliver my line."

"It's the real deal," she says, but she gives it to him anyway.

"Otherwise, musty old books can get a little dull."

She laughs. He opens the book.

"They threw out the last page as irrelevant to the authenticity analysis, but maybe it's not irrelevant to you." He turns past all the blank pages to the very end of the book. Written in modern ink on the final page is a single line.

Benito lived happily ever after in the pages of this book.

Alice smiles. Daylet smiles, watching her.

"Did you write that?" he asked, half-joking.

"No, I would never destroy a world treasure with the graffiti of my humble musings!" she says with a slight sarcasm. Then, she nods slowly. "A very precocious twelve-year-old wrote it. I recognize the handwriting. I read a lot of school papers."

Daylet chuckles as the bell in the cathedral across the street begins to toll.

"So do I."

Peter Michaels slowly awakes from his coma. The bell, across the sea, continues to toll. He looks around the room, and out the window, he sees a Boston cathedral instead.

Taryn is asleep in a chair with her homemade book in her arms.

"Taryn?"

Taryn wakes groggily, and when she does, she sees her dad. She lights up like she never has before. She wraps her arms around him and squeezes so tightly she thinks that he'll burst.

Peter can't remember much of anything from his time in the coma, but being reunited with Taryn is the most incredible moment of his life. He squeezes her right back, as much as he can, unsure if he'll ever be able to tell her everything he's thinking.

Back at the University, Alice points to the cathedral drawing in the book, so Daylet holds it up. They see together that it's the same as the one across from them.

"There's so much history here that we can connect with in the present. I think you really have an eye for it." He looks her in the eyes as he speaks to her. "I had a word with the Chairman down there between cheese cubes. Even though this book might not be the definitive literary discovery since the Dead Sea Scrolls, your ambition and imagination impressed us. Me. It impresses me. It would be an honor to squeeze you into my class here in Seville in the fall. Congratulations, you're in the program."

She can't keep herself from leaping towards him and giving him a hug. "Thank you!" The release is slightly awkward, but she doesn't even care. "Will Tim be your TA next year?"

"Yep," Daylet says with a funny smile and an expression that's difficult to read. "Until he graduates. Whenever that might be. He's been with us for four years. He's often a bit…in his head, I'd say…but he's a good kid."

Alice nods with a smile. "You just can't give up on those."

When Alice returns to the States, Peter is still in the hospital. Alice decides it best that she pay him and Taryn a personal visit. When she arrives, she sets the book on the empty bedside table for Taryn. Then, she turns and smiles at Peter. It's a bit awkward, considering his position, but she won't run away from this.

"I'm sorry to intrude," she says. "I'm Alice Loureiro, Taryn's Spanish teacher."

"Of course." Peter nods in recognition. "We had a parent-teacher meeting."

"I am so truly relieved that you are doing so well. I'm embarrassed to be here. It's probably uncomfortable to be gushed over by a near-stranger."

The pair share a light laugh.

"Not at all," the man says. "There was less gushing from the people I half-expected it from, so I don't mind it at all.

Taryn is the closest person to my heart, and you two seem to have a history."

Alice turns to Taryn then, who is nestled up against her father's arm. Taryn straightens up at Alice's presence.

"I brought your book back," she whispers. "Thank you for…thank you. It changed my life."

"That's okay," Taryn says with a shrug. "I wrote my own."

Taryn smiles, and Alice is quite relieved. "I'd love to read it."

"I'm sure you would," Taryn teases. She's met with a laugh from her teacher.

"So," Peter clears his throat and raises his volume slightly. "You just flew back from Seville?"

"Yes!" Alice has so much to say about it that she can hardly keep quiet.

"I've been many times. History really is alive there."

Alice nods enthusiastically. "I'm going back actually. To explore for the summer and then start a graduate program in the fall."

"Wow." Peter gives her a smile.

"How was it?!" Taryn's attention is immediately piqued. "Dad never tells me enough!"

Peter looks at Taryn with such love and mischief. "Maybe it's time for you to see for yourself.

She's elated and breaks into a restrained grin.

Alice sits in the airport. It is a place of excitement and hope now that she's here on her own terms. Peter and Taryn happily share a pretzel nearby, Peter's arm is still in a sling. They all share an excited smile. Taryn offers Alice a chunk of pretzel, but she declines.

APRIL 22, 1616

Dear Will,

I woke up today so tired, but light. I knew I would set aside my pen today once and for all. I'm not sure what this is I've written of myself. I won't print this one. It belongs to the universe now. It is one thing to write as a poet and another to write as a historian. The poet can recount or sing about things not as they were, but as they should have been, and the historian must write about them as they were, without adding or subtracting anything from the truth. I am neither poet nor historian. I am only a purveyor of my own thoughts.

I am Benito. I am Miguel.

For me alone, Don Quixote was born, and I for him. He was a man of action. I was merely his scribe, you understand. I imagine our words will live beyond us, in new worlds and minds.

But I have a feeling we are finally falling asleep to this world, with her wars and love and honor. I watched my mother sever from her only child, the explosions in Florida, the Turkish boy who ran to his mother's arms, Don Juan and all his windmill battles in Antwerp.

In this sleep of death, what dreams may come? Let us fly to other wonders that we know not of. We are beginning anew. Our tales and truths will stay behind. Whether they are history or fantasy is up to the reader. Our words belong to them now.

Adventure awaits, my friend!

- Miguel de Cerbantes Saavedra

In the heart of Seville, Alice and her travel companions are visiting Cervantes' memorial. Her attention is drawn toward the sky. With wonder, she squints to see better in the sunlight. Taryn and Peter look up too.

Small white flecks get bigger and bigger as they float down over Cervantes' statue. Alice holds out her hand and a snowflake falls in her palm. Regular snow lightly, magically falls around the three, sparkling in the sun. The statue is lightly dusted in white.

They have never known such silence and tranquility.